Sons of a Parisian Dynasty

*Claiming their legacy. Finding their family.
Meeting their match!*

With the retirement of their patriarch, the renowned Causcelle triplets are taking over an aristocratic empire! These gorgeous yet media-shy billionaires are stepping into the spotlight to make their mark on Paris.

Firstborn Nic has taken over the hotel branch of the business—and immediately caused a scandal with the company's new attorney! While Raoul is heading up the rest of the corporation—at least until mysteriously absent Jean-Louis can be found...

But while these brooding siblings are taking the business world by storm, their hearts are completely off-limits—when you're this wealthy, love always comes with a catch, right? Until they meet the women who show them just how wrong they are!

Find out who tames Nic in
Capturing the CEO's Guarded Heart

Available now!

And look out for Jean-Louis's and Raoul's stories

Coming soon!

Dear Reader,

In the past I've written about twins, but this new series, Sons of a Parisian Dynasty, is the story of triplet brothers. I've never known or met anyone who's a triplet. I've had to use my imagination to get inside their psyches to understand how they feel and react to being part of a set. I've had a lot of fun working out their stories, their struggles, their triumphs, their loves. I hope you'll like this first book, *Capturing the CEO's Guarded Heart*. It is here you'll meet Nicolas Causcelle, known as Nic. He is the triplet who was born first in that amazing birth.

Enjoy!

Rebecca Winters

Capturing the CEO's Guarded Heart

Rebecca Winters

HARLEQUIN

Romance

Recycling programs
for this product may
not exist in your area.

ISBN-13: 978-1-335-73680-2

Capturing the CEO's Guarded Heart

Copyright © 2022 by Rebecca Winters

Harlequin Enterprises ULC
22 Adelaide St. West, 41st Floor
Toronto, Ontario M5H 4E3, Canada
www.Harlequin.com

Printed in U.S.A.

Rebecca Winters lives in Salt Lake City, Utah. With canyons and high alpine meadows full of wildflowers, she never runs out of places to explore. They, plus her favorite vacation spots in Europe, often end up as backgrounds for her romance novels—because writing is her passion, along with her family and church. Rebecca loves to hear from readers. If you wish to email her, please visit her website at rebeccawinters.net.

Books by Rebecca Winters

Harlequin Romance

The Baldasseri Royals

Reclaiming the Prince's Heart
Falling for the Baldasseri Prince
Second Chance with His Princess

Secrets of a Billionaire

The Greek's Secret Heir
Unmasking the Secret Prince

Escape to Provence

Falling for Her French Tycoon
Falling for His Unlikely Cinderella

The Princess Brides

How to Propose to a Princess

Visit the Author Profile page
at Harlequin.com for more titles.

Dedicated to my dear siblings. I came from a family of six children, five girls and one boy. Everyone should have come from a family of six siblings as marvelous and great as mine.

Praise for
Rebecca Winters

"This is the first book that I have read by this author but definitely not the last as it is an amazing story. I definitely recommend this book as it is so well written and definitely worth reading."

—*Goodreads* on *How to Propose to a Princess*

CHAPTER ONE

THE PARISIAN JUDGE of the Third Civil Division—the man otherwise referred to as President of the Land Court—tapped his gavel.

"In the case of Causcelle vs. Mercier, the court finds for the plaintiff."

Yes!

"The defendant will pay the penalties for fraud. If opposing chief counsels will meet with me in chambers, this court is adjourned."

Thank you, Monsieur President.

Anelise Lavigny had won her first case for the Causcelle Corporation and couldn't be happier. Soon she would call her father, Hugo Lavigny, and tell him the good news. Three years ago her father had become good friends with the world-famous Louis Causcelle. Apparently they'd met through business, but she'd never learned why their relationship had become so important to him.

After graduating from law school, she'd gotten her start working as an attorney in her father's office. He was known for developing polymers and electronics. Yet she'd only been working for her father a few months when Louis Causcelle came to her father's business and offered her a position at his corporation. She would be one of the attorneys for the hotel division. The Causcelle empire was worth billions and had been touted as one of the top five that drove the French economy.

Her parents immediately urged her to consider joining Louis's corporation. They told her they thought it was an honor that Louis had sought her out. Her parents assured her she'd be an asset at Causcelle.

In a way their encouragement had surprised her because they'd been very protective of her since the death of her fiancé. They'd done everything to show her their love and shield her from the intrusive press since her father was a prominent man. She'd leaned on their support. It went without saying that because she was their only child, they'd all been very close. Maybe a little too much?

Winning the case today had given her more confidence that she'd made the right decision to work for Louis Causcelle. Anelise had to admit to a surge of excitement at becoming more independent. She liked the feeling and enjoyed living on her own.

Serge Thibault, the chief attorney in Causcelle's hotel division and her immediate boss, nodded to her that she should leave without him because he'd be a while. Under the circumstances she'd go to her apartment to eat before she went back to the office.

Anelise left the courtroom of the Palais de Justice with her briefcase and headed for the company limo waiting for her across the Boulevard du Palais bridge.

A delightful May afternoon brought out the usual hundreds of tourists visiting the Ile de la Cité, where the Palais de Justice was located in the heart of Paris.

The boat-shaped island in the middle of the Seine River contained much of the history of the city of lights. Never could she forget she was walking over the ground of the former royal residence of the kings of France. One could still visit the Sainte-

Chapelle, built in the thirteenth century by King Saint Louis. The sacred place was known for its exquisite stained-glass windows portraying Biblical scenes. So much history...

She savored her surroundings as she climbed in the limo and asked the chauffeur to take her to her apartment in the Marais area of Paris. It contained the gorgeous stone buildings and cobblestone streets that made her feel she was living in a more romantic time in France. The Causcelle family owned several properties there. One was a sprawling, former two-story royal palace that had become their corporate headquarters.

A block away stood another former royal palace that had been modernized. Various members of the large Causcelle family lived there at times, including Louis Causcelle when he was in town. A staffed kitchen provided their meals. Louis called it the *palais*.

He'd insisted that Anelise stay in the vacant suite on the main floor where his eldest daughter stayed when she came to Paris. Louis had insisted Anelise move there, so she only had to walk a short distance to work. Otherwise, she'd have to commute for a half hour from her parents' home in the posh sixteenth arrondissement.

Joy, joy.

After losing Andre Navarre in a fatal car crash eighteen months ago, she hadn't thought she could be happy again. He'd brought such love into her life, for him to have died at the scene had sent her into shock for days. She withdrew from people and hadn't wanted to finish law school. Her dreams of being Andre's wife and working with him when they traveled had died with him. Her darling Andre who'd just graduated in engineering no longer existed.

The media had exploited the crash because she was the daughter of multimillionaire Hugo Lavigny. They'd intruded in her life, even speculated that his death might have ended a promising career in law for her because of her heartache. But they callously suggested that it didn't matter because she would inherit her father's money one day.

When Anelise had read those cruel, disgusting words, she'd been sickened and angered by them. How dared they? That comment roused her out of her grief long enough to finish up her degree, but many nights she'd cried, most of them longing for him.

Thankfully enough time had passed since then that she didn't feel that way today. This new position at Causcelle had pulled her from that dark place and given her fresh focus. Ferreting out the fraud in the Mercier case meant Louis Causcelle wouldn't regret hiring her. Not yet anyway. Not if she could help it.

Her limo driver drove her through the courtyard, past the fountain and around the side to the main entrance. She got out, thanking him before she hurried past two more security guards and entered the building.

A fiftyish male guard at the front desk of the entrance monitored who went in and out. She couldn't help but notice an attractive brunette having a heated conversation with him. Something was wrong.

The flustered man nodded to Anelise. "Your father called and hopes you'll phone him when you can, Mademoiselle Lavigny."

That's right. She'd turned off her cell in court. Her parents, especially her dad, were anxious to know how her first case had gone. "*Merci*, Guy. I'll do it now." Anelise started walking down the hall to her suite when she heard footsteps behind her.

"Wait, Mademoiselle Lavigny!"

She turned around as the other woman hurried toward her. Anelise thought she recognized her as a French television star featured in some drama series. She couldn't recall its name or that of the actress.

The *vedette*'s brown eyes with long dark lashes did a quick inventory of Anelise. "I take it you live here."

"Yes."

"How did you accomplish *that*?" She folded her arms like a schoolteacher waiting for an explanation from her naughty student. It sounded like the woman wanted to move in here. Guy must have told her she would have to be invited. Anelise was surprised the star hadn't asked her agent to help her.

The more she thought about it, the more she wondered why this woman felt she had a right to access an apartment here. This place existed strictly for the Causcelle family and their friends. Maybe the woman *was* a friend. A very special friend, like a former lover of one of the Causcelle men perhaps?

One finely arched brow lifted. "In other words, you won't tell me."

Good heavens. The woman really was upset. "I don't know what it is you want."

"A suite, of course, but the man at the front desk is no help."

"This isn't a hotel. I'm afraid you would have to talk to the head of the Causcelle Corporation."

"Is that what *you* did?" Her peremptory attitude might explain why Guy had seemed out of sorts. "Isn't he as old and impossible as Methuselah?"

Not Louis Causcelle. He was young at heart. Anelise liked him very much, but none of this was her business. "He's a wonderful man. If you'll excuse me, I need to make a phone call."

The minute Anelise entered her apartment, she ordered room service and freshened up, then called her dad at his office to explain what had happened in court.

"As you know, I discovered that the agent for the Mercier Company failed to transfer the stock certificates in a timely manner following the merger with Causcelle. The discovery resulted in a six-million-euro settlement for us."

"That's my daughter! I'm so proud of you I could burst."

She'd never heard him so happy. "Thanks, Papa. I'm pretty excited about it too."

"What's the rest of your day like?"

"I'm going back to work, but I'll be over tonight to see you and Maman. *A bientôt.*"

The landline rang as Nic Causcelle emerged from the shower in his suite at the *palais*. He'd just flown into Paris on the company jet from Chalon Champforgeuil in eastern France. It was the closest airport to the Causcelle ancestral home in La Racineuse fifteen miles away. His father, Louis, had become ill and would be living there from now on where his married daughters and their families would take care of him.

As for Nic, his father had put him in charge of Causcelle Hotels, a job he didn't relish. He much preferred continuing to work with his brother Raoul in the other divisions of the corporation here in Paris. They included exports, manufacturing, luxury cars and a trucking firm. But with their other brother, Jean-Louis, having left the family ten years ago to serve in the military, it meant either Nic or Raoul would be required to head the hotel business from now on.

Their father had flipped a coin. Nic called heads, Raoul tails. Up came heads. Raoul wasn't happy about it either. The two brothers were thicker than proverbial thieves and enjoyed working together. Nic couldn't understand why his father didn't ask their cousin Pascal to take over, but it didn't happen. At least Nic and Raoul would do business in the same place. And they both slept here in the *palais* so they could see each other, but only coming and going, unless they arranged for time off to be together.

He walked over to the phone and picked up. *"Oui?"*

"Pardon, Nicolas. Welcome back. It's Guy in the lobby. Mademoiselle Lafrenière has just been here asking about you again. She'd like to move in here. I told her that wasn't possible. It's not the first time she has asked, if you know what I mean."

Unfortunately, Nic *did* know.

"She thought you were coming back to Paris last week and has been here every day to inquire. She expects a call from you."

His dark brows furrowed. "Do you have the number?"

"Yes."

"Give it to me and I'll take care of it. *Merci*, Guy."

Once that was done, he hung up. Babette Lafrenière. That was all he needed. An ac-

tress with stars in her eyes and so ambitious,
it oozed out of her. He'd met her over a month
ago at one of their car dealerships while he'd
gone there to straighten out a managerial
problem.

The middle-aged manager, Pierre, always
went overboard when Nic or Raoul met with
him. On this day he was so dazzled by the
TV star who'd come to look at the luxury
cars, he couldn't contain himself introduc-
ing her to Nic. The second she set eyes on
him, she ignored the manager and wanted
Nic to do the honors of helping her with her
purchase.

She had a brazen side to her nature, asking
him to take her for a ride in the Bugatti she'd
decided to buy. Her exotic kind of beauty
couldn't be ignored, but her hunger for everything turned him off and he excused himself.

Somehow—perhaps through the car manager—she'd found out where he lived. Poor
Guy at the desk had been haunted by her
phone calls and visits ever since. Nic needed
to do something about it today, but would
leave it until after he'd been to the office
where his father had worked for years. Once
he'd said hello to everyone in his capacity

as their new CEO over Causcelle Hotels, he would call Mademoiselle Lafrenière and say something that would put her off for good.

After dressing in a suit and tie, he left the *palais* and started walking to the office. A way off he noticed a light brown-haired woman with slender curves in a two-piece dark blue business suit headed in the same direction. She carried a briefcase and her hair had been caught back in a tortoiseshell clip, but he couldn't see her face.

Something unique about her had drawn his attention. She walked with a spring in her step on those long legs of hers, seemingly excited, maybe happy even because it was Friday. How would it be to feel like that?

To his surprise she entered the Causcelle Corporation and went right up the stairs as if she knew exactly where she was going. More curious than ever, he didn't use the private entrance with the elevator that took him straight to his office. Instead he walked behind her to the hotel division that took up the whole second floor. She entered the reception area of the front office and shut the door.

Within seconds Nic opened it quietly and heard the voice of George Delong, the executive assistant to Nic's father for years. The

man could run the place blindfolded. *"Bon
après-midi,* Anelise. Any good news?"

"We won!"

"Felicitations!"

"Merci."

"Where's Serge?"

"Talking with the judge."

His gray brows lifted above his glasses.
"While you've been gone, our new boss has
come back from his vacation in La Racineuse."

"New? What do you mean? Where's Monsieur Causcelle?"

Nic came all the way in. "I'm right here."

She wheeled around, catching him off
guard because she was lovelier than he
could have imagined. Her sea-glass blue eyes
stared at him out of an oval face that needed
no makeup.

George got to his feet looking surprised
that Nic had appeared at all. "Mademoiselle
Lavigny, may I present Nicolas Causcelle,
the new CEO of Causcelle Hotels and son
of Louis Causcelle."

Lavigny? It all made sense. She had to
be the daughter of Louis's friend Hugo, the
one he'd mentioned the other day back in La
Racineuse. Nic thought back to his father's

friendship with the other man. Odd how none of their family had ever met Hugo, but Nic's father kept his cards close to the chest on occasion.

Since Nic had called off his engagement to Denise Fournette two years ago, Nic's father had been urging him to find the right woman next time and get married. But Nic didn't trust his own judgment where permanent relationships were concerned, and those words had fallen on deaf ears.

For some reason his father had hired Hugo's daughter to work here once his doctor had told him he must retire. Nic had the suspicion something was going on he didn't understand. Why had his father suddenly decided on *her*? No doubt she had the right qualifications, but he had to admit to being curious.

"Mademoiselle Lavigny? It's a pleasure to meet you."

"And mine, monsieur." She acted all business.

"If you'll come with me to my office, we'll get acquainted." He turned to his father's assistant. "It's good to see you, George. We'll talk Monday morning after I meet with Serge."

"Tres bien."
"Bon weekend."

Anelise followed the attractive man who constituted one of the amazing Causcelle identical triplet sons born twenty-nine years ago. Their births had made headlines throughout France and Europe. They'd been famous from day one for being children of the foremost billionaire in France.

His sons would inherit everything Louis Causcelle owned, from hotels, transport services, trucking chains and elite cars to manufacturing companies. Their photos were constantly in the media and newspapers, but she'd never met one of them in person. She found that odd. Why hadn't Louis ever introduced his children to her parents?

According to Anelise's father, the triplets had been courted by royalty throughout Europe. They came from an old aristocratic family with property in eastern France deeded to their family back in the 1200s by Philip II. Their genealogy made them a source of great envy and constant targets of publicity.

The fact that they were handsome as Adonis and unmarried would make them desirable to every female, available or not. But no male possessed her deceased fiancé's dark blond looks and green eyes. Just remembering him brought a pang to her heart. She had to keep fighting this longing when she thought of him in order to maintain a professional front in front of the staff and now her new boss.

Anelise walked past the suite where she worked. Through another door she saw the other attorney, Helene Garnier, a woman in her fifties Anelise had met through Louis. She liked the older woman Louis had praised. Moving on, they entered the suite at the end of the hall where Louis had interviewed her after hiring her, but the moment was surreal.

The tall, solidly built male with wavy black hair led her to his inner sanctum. He indicated a chair for her and sat down at the desk where his father had once reigned. His vibrant black eyes missed nothing as they studied her beneath equally dark brows.

To think this son was now the head of the hotel division where she worked... Anelise couldn't comprehend it. He didn't know her from Adam. Now that she'd done well on her first case, she'd felt on a little firmer ground with Louis Causcelle, but no longer.

"My father was worried about the Mercier case, but evidently you found the lie in the details in time to stop the merger. I couldn't help but overhear you tell George you won your case. That will please my father."

"Thank you. He's been very kind to me. Would you please tell me what has happened that he's no longer the head?"

Nic sat forward. "Does that bother you?"

She didn't look away. "Frankly, I'm very disappointed. I was looking forward to working for him. My father says he's such a brilliant man and I'd learn so much."

"He isn't happy about leaving the company either, but he has a bad heart and is on medication. The doctor insisted he retire and stay home with our married sisters and the rest of our extended family."

"I'm so sorry. Is it permanent?"

"I'm afraid so."

She lowered her head. "How sad. I enjoyed our meeting before he hired me a month ago."

"I'll let him know about your triumph today."

"Thank you."

"Mademoiselle Lavigny, do you mind if I ask you what convinced you to join our corporation, other than our fathers' friendship?"

"Oh, not at all. I was keen for a fresh environment after working for my father's company. You know, something new and challenging. Th-that's what I've been needing," she stammered.

"My father told me you lost your fiancé. How long ago?"

"Over nineteen months now."

"I'm very sorry."

"So am I, but I've been making a new life for myself. This job offer thrilled me because the Causcelle Corporation has always had a brilliant reputation. But it's more than that. Your father came to my father's company to talk to me and I was so surprised. When I met him, he was so charming and personable, I felt like we became instant friends. He can tell a tale like no one else, and he drew me out of myself.

"When I told him about my life growing up without siblings, he pulled a photo out of his wallet and showed it to me. He said, 'Try living with these!' It turned out to be a picture of you and your brothers. You stood there in a pasture in shorts and tops with a cow near you."

"He *showed* you that photo?" The man sounded surprised.

"Yes, and I can understand why. I've never seen cuter three-year-old boys who all looked exactly alike. I told him I would have loved some brothers like that. He spoke fondly about your older sisters too, and he teared up when he talked about all of you.

"I told him my mother couldn't have more children after I came along, but she'd wanted a large family like his. He began to weep and wished your mother had been alive to see how wonderfully you've all turned out. If ever a father loved his family, he loves you. Do you mind telling me where that picture was taken?"

After a long silence he said, "Near the Causcelle Fromagerie. It's located on an ancient piece of property near the family château in La Racineuse where we raise Montbeliarde cows for cheese making."

"Like that cow I saw in the background of the picture?"

"Exactly. Those are the red-and-white pied cattle used for dairying and cheese making from the Haute-Saône/Doubs region of France. They descend from the Bernoise cattle. Did you know they were brought into France in the eighteenth century by the Mennonites?"

"I had no idea."

"Those cows produced milk that made the cheese my great-great-great-grandfather Auguste first sold at market. Cheese was the first product of the family business."

She couldn't hear enough. "The beginning of everything! No wonder my father always insists on buying Causcelle cheese. I love it too."

"That's true loyalty. My father would be delighted to hear it."

"What was the second product?"

"You mean he didn't tell you after your long conversation?"

"No." She chuckled. "But I could have listened to him all day if he'd had the time."

He eyed her through narrowed lids, as if he were trying to figure her out. "Auguste rode his horse to market to sell the cheese. When he'd made enough money over the years, he bought a cart to carry more cheese. Rather than a product, you could say that his method was the precursor to the trucking business his son Francois began to develop in eastern France."

"And so on and so forth down through the years to the present." She smiled at him.

"What is *your* contribution to this chain of remarkable events?"

When the light went out of his eyes, Anelise knew at once her question had brought an abrupt end to their conversation. His hard, chiseled jaw tautened. "It stopped with my brothers and me."

"How can you say that after what I've learned about all of you?"

His eyes had clouded over, confusing her. "The story isn't fully written yet, is it?"

"You mean—" Anelise stopped, suddenly feeling terrible. "Forgive me if I touched on something so personal for you. When your father talked about his family, he spoke with such pride."

"But?" he questioned, surprising her. "You didn't finish what you were going to say."

"It doesn't matter."

"I think it does."

She took a deep breath. "I'd rather not."

"Please. I'd like to hear."

"He conveyed such a sadness over your brother who joined the military. Forgive me for saying anything."

"No problem. Go on. I want to hear it all."

Anelise feared she'd made a mistake mentioning the photo. She sensed a well of sorrow in him. "He told me he'd been so upset when your brother joined the military, it caused an estrangement that never healed. He sounded heartbroken about it. After he'd wept, he admitted it was his one of his many regrets that he hadn't been kind to him when he signed up."

She stopped for breath. "He wished he'd had the chance to beg his forgiveness, but feared it was too late." Anelise hadn't known Louis was seriously ill when he'd hired her, but she did now and it all made sense. Louis had feared dying before seeing his son again. "Before our interview was over, your father prophesied that each of his sons would take the Causcelle Corporation to new heights. Of that I have no doubt."

Her words seemed to have affected Nicolas Causcelle in ways she didn't understand. His silence had turned into brooding and a frown appeared, as if he were upset. Again she felt sadness radiate from him and his reaction made her uneasy. Perhaps he wanted to be alone. She stood up.

"I apologize for taking your time. Please know I'm truly honored to be working for your company. Please give your father my best. Tell him I'll miss him and the talks I would have enjoyed."

Anelise turned and exited his office. Whatever had been bothering him lay deep seated inside him. She wished she knew what had troubled him. When she reached the front desk at the other end of the hall, she was astonished to see the same self-absorbed woman who'd confronted her earlier at the *palais*.

The TV star standing at George's desk stared at Anelise with a stunned expression. "What are *you* doing here?" The woman's rudeness was off the charts.

George got to his feet. "Mademoiselle Lafrenière, may I introduce you to Mademoiselle Lavigny, one of our new corporate attorneys."

Shock registered. "*You're* an attorney?"

Anelise smiled. "It's a surprise to me too." She turned to George. "We met earlier today. Now I can put a name to her face."

"Mademoiselle Lafrenière is an actress you may have seen on the *Paris Noir* TV series," he informed her.

She eyed the other woman. "How exciting for you, mademoiselle. I'm sorry, but I don't watch much television. Now, if you'll excuse

me, I have work to do before I leave." Anelise
felt the other woman stare daggers at her as
she turned to go to her office down the hall.
More than ever she sensed this woman had
been in a relationship with one of the Causcelle sons. She just didn't know which one.

CHAPTER TWO

NIC HADN'T MOVED a muscle since Mademoiselle Lavigny had left his office. With furrowed brows, he thought over the conversation with the new and beautiful young attorney. More curious about her than ever, he looked up her résumé on their personnel file. She was twenty-six and would be married by now if her fiancé hadn't been killed.

Interesting... His father knew how to manipulate better than anyone he knew. Had he decided to dangle her under Nic's nose with marriage the outcome? Why not hire her to work under Nic? Clever. He had to admit she was tempting bait, but no way would he allow that to happen!

Her faint flowery fragrance still lingered in the air...subtle, but there.

A part of him didn't want to believe his parent would endeavor to play cupid with him and Mademoiselle Lavigny. But after meeting her face-to-face, Nic realized his father had been so enchanted by her, he'd confided in her regarding very private family matters that included his mother. He'd even told her about his regrets over the way he'd treated Jean-Louis. He'd even wept in front of her, yet he'd always been such a private person around most people.

Nic's father had never talked to him or Raoul about his sorrow at hurting their brother. Had her engaging personality prompted his father to be open because she was a naturally friendly person who invited confidences? Maybe her warmth reminded him of his friend Hugo and he felt close to her because of it.

What was it between his father and hers that had bonded the two men three years ago? Did she know something Nic didn't, and was more than willing to try and seduce him for Louis's sake? If so, she made a superb actress. But after his mistake in getting engaged to Denise, he couldn't deal with another relationship. As for Mademoiselle Lafrenière…

Now would be the time to phone the annoying starlet and get this over with. But as he reached for the landline phone, George buzzed him. In a low voice he said, "Nicolas? There's a Mademoiselle Lafrenière here to see your father."

My father?

"I told her to be seated. She says she's a friend of yours."

Speak of the devil. His hand tightened on the receiver. "She isn't a friend of mine or our family. Tell her my father has retired and send her on her way. I'll call her later."

"Tres bien."

Nic hung up and left the office through the private elevator to the rear exit of the *palais*. After the short walk to his living quarters, he phoned the starlet on the *palais* line that had to go through the switchboard. He left a message for her to call. A half hour later Guy told him she was on the other line. He thanked him and clicked on.

"This is Monsieur Causcelle."

"At last. I was beginning to wonder if I'd ever hear from you, Monsieur Causcelle. Or can I call you Nic?"

Enough of her pointless flirting. "I've been out of town."

"So I understand. You're a hard man to track down. Since you're back, let's have drinks together. It's a Friday night and I don't have plans. Anywhere you say."

Nic suppressed an epithet. "I'm afraid that would be impossible. I'm permanently involved with someone else." It was the one statement he felt would put her off, even if it wasn't true.

"Ooh, that sounds serious."

"Very."

"It wouldn't be you've gone back to your former fiancée after all this time, would it? Or is this woman the formidable young attorney at Causcelle Headquarters who has brought you to your knees?"

Formidable? An interesting choice of words. What did the starlet know about Mademoiselle Lavigny? He closed his eyes in quiet fury. "I hope you're enjoying your new car, Mademoiselle Lafrenière. Best of luck in your career."

He hung up, not giving her a chance to say anything else, and phoned his brother's office on the main floor at Causcelle's. Nic needed to talk to him about his conversation with Mademoiselle Lavigny.

Raoul's assistant told him his brother was on the phone with a client. Nic left the message that he had arrived home and hoped Raoul would come by after he left work.

A half hour later, there was a familiar knock on the door of Nic's suite. "Come on in, *frerot*."

Raoul appeared. They gave each other a bear hug before sitting down in the living room.

"How does it feel to walk in the old man's shoes?"

Nic eyed his brother. "Weird. I'll never get used to the idea and prefer working with you the way we always have."

"I don't like it either."

"It's been a strange day and I haven't even lived through the first one yet. Do you remember our father telling you that he'd hired a new attorney?"

"You must mean his friend Hugo's daughter. He mentioned it to me on the phone."

Nic blinked. "That's the one."

"I take it you met her."

"Yes. She'd just returned from court. It seems she won her first case."

"That'll please Papa. What's she like?"

He rubbed the back of his neck where the nerves bunched up. "I'm still trying to figure her out."

"I guess you know our father invited her to live here at the *palais*."

"He *what*?" Nic shot to his feet. "I've been in and out of Paris on business and know nothing about that."

"Mademoiselle Lavigny has been here for the last month. Corinne told me because Papa invited her to move into Corinne's suite. I thought you must have known."

No. Their oldest married sister hadn't said a word. Was that on purpose because she was in on their father's plan to get Nic married off? Nic had been the first triplet born, and still single. "So, Mademoiselle Lavigny is living downstairs…"

"As far as I know."

It made sense. "That's why I saw her walking to headquarters earlier." *In the same direction as himself and giving off vibes that had drawn his attention.*

"Well? Aren't you going to tell me about her?"

"How much time do you have?"

"I have no plans for tonight." Raoul flicked him a curious glance. "You seem upset, Nic. What's going on?"

"More than you know. Today I believe I've seen the fruition of a well-thought-out, ingenious plot our father has been working on since I broke off with Denise. But there's more, much more. It has to do with Papa and Jean-Louis."

"Now you've really got me curious."

After Nic called the kitchen, he related to his brother what he'd learned.

"Papa actually *told* her about his fight with Jean-Louis?"

Nic nodded. "She said he wept over it and would give anything to ask his forgiveness, but feared it was too late and he'd never see him again."

Bewildered, Raoul got to his feet. "I didn't know father was suffering over it. He's never said a word to me."

"Nor me."

"Why would he tell Mademoiselle Lavigny something so personal? I don't get it."

'I don't either. I'm going to phone Corinne and find out if he told her or our other sisters." Nic pulled his cell phone from his jacket pocket.

"Good idea. Put it on speaker."

The two of them talked to their eldest sister, who swore neither she nor their sisters knew anything, but in a way, she was glad he was suffering. "Jean-Louis didn't want to work for the family business and took a way out by joining the military. Papa should have understood."

"Agreed," Nic murmured. "Do you ever hear from him beyond the once-a-year Christmas card with no address that we all get?"

"You know better than to ask me that. How about you and Raoul? Has he shared something with you because you're his blood brothers in every sense of the word? We sisters aren't his triplet siblings. Jean-Louis is as bad as Papa in the Sphinx department."

Corinne had that right. The Sphinx was always inscrutable. They'd all been hurt by his ten years of silence. "Just once I wish he would break down."

"I miss him and know you do too, Nic. Wish we could talk longer, but I've got to go. Papa is calling for me. Talk to you soon."

"Thanks, Corinne. Give him our love. Let us know if there's anything you need." Nic clicked off and stared at his brother. "Are you thinking what I'm thinking?"

Raoul nodded. "The doctor says Papa is on a downward spiral. We should try to contact Jean-Louis and let him know about his condition before it gets worse."

"Since he's never answered our mail or emails, I think we should hire a private detective to find out exactly where he's serving and get word to him while there's still time. Serge has contacts and will know the right person for the job."

"Let's call him now, but tell him we don't want Papa to know what we're doing."

"D'accord."

Nic phoned Serge, who gave him the name of Claude Giraud, a man who'd been in the French secret service and would know how to trace their brother. Once the call had been made, they waited for him to come to the hotel and meet with them in Nic's suite.

"We appreciate your coming on such short notice," Raoul spoke first. "Our brother has been away from the family ten years. He's purposely stayed away and you need to know why. He didn't want anything to do with our family business."

Nic joined in. "We've been known as the triumvirate all our lives and are always in the news. Jean-Louis couldn't take it and we don't blame him for his feelings since we feel the same way. The combination of relentless media exposure, intrusion into our private lives and being treated as if we were all one and the same person was too much for him."

Monsieur Giraud nodded. "So, he joined the military to get away."

"Yes, but our father couldn't handle it from the beginning. He had dreams for the three of us, but Jean-Louis dropped out of business college in Paris where we were all studying. He threatened to join the army and Papa almost had a coronary, but that didn't stop our brother. He left for good and the two of them have been estranged ever since."

Claude shook his head. "How tragic."

"Yes," Raoul agreed. "The silence has been very effective. We don't know where he's deployed, let alone how to get word to him. Our mail goes to an official military mailing address. We'll give you that address. He's never answered one letter we've sent over the years."

"We receive a yearly Christmas card from him, and that's it," Nic supplied. "Now the situation has grown serious because our father is ill and the doctor says he won't recover. Raoul and I want Jean-Louis to know Papa is grieving over the pain he caused ten years ago. I know in my gut our brother has been suffering too. If you can locate him for us, we'll be forever in your debt."

"Money is no object," Raoul added in a solemn tone.

"Be assured I'll do everything possible. I'll let you know the instant I have the news you're waiting for. Do you know the date he joined the army?"

"October fifth or sixth, ten years ago."

"Possibly from Paris. That gives me a starting point. I'll find him."

"Thank you," they said sotto voce.

After Claude left, Nic turned to his brother. "Why don't I order dinner for both of us? Then I want to talk some more about Mademoiselle Lavigny."

Anelise studied the next case sitting on her desk and decided to ponder it over the weekend. An hour later she left headquarters and walked to the *palais* to reach her trusty blue Peugeot in the rear parking area. Her parents were expecting her.

She got in and wound around to the courtyard, where she saw a red Bugatti. It didn't surprise her that the TV star sat at the wheel obviously waiting for someone. No doubt that had to be Nic Causcelle or his brother

Raoul. Louis had told her both his sons lived here at the *palais*.

Anelise drove past her and turned onto the street headed for her parents' home in Passy. She loved its cobblestoned streets and tucked-away museums.

Later over dinner she told her parents everything that happened after she left court. "I have to admit I'm shocked that Louis has been forced to retire."

Her father shook his head. "It doesn't surprise me. He's worked nonstop for years to build up his corporation and should have slowed down a year ago. Now he's put his son Nicolas in charge. What do you think of him?"

"I'm afraid the more pertinent question would be what he thinks of me."

Her mother Anne cocked her head. "Why do you say that, darling? You won your first case. That should have impressed him."

"He complimented me. If only I hadn't said anything else."

"Explain yourself," her father interjected.

"Oh, I made the mistake of telling him how much I loved the photograph of the triplets his father showed me from his wallet. It was too personal a remark and I'm afraid it might have upset him."

"In what way?" Her mother sounded perplexed.

"I asked him about the cow in the photo, and that comment led me to pose more questions about the beginnings of the Causcelle empire. It was then I felt a sadness coming from him. Maybe I had intruded too much and he regrets having to work with me."

Her father shook his head. "Nonsense. Something else has to be going on with him. Kind of like the way you sometimes get when someone asks you about Andre." Anelise knew her father was right about that. "Nicolas is too aware of his father's shrewd business sense in hiring you to question it. Give the office politics time."

"You're right." She got up from the table. "I've learned one thing. Never get into anything personal with him again."

"Then you're happy to be there?"

"I hope I will be, Papa."

Her mother looked concerned. "You sound exhausted."

"I am. It was a long day at court. Thank you for dinner and always listening to me."

They'd had to do too much of that, and it was long past time she functioned on her own.

She gave both of them a hug, then hurried out of their home to her car. As she drove, she thought she noticed a red Bugatti a few cars behind her. Traffic was heavy, but it might be the same one she'd seen in the *palais* courtyard.

Anelise eventually arrived and pulled around to park. Through the rearview mirror she saw the red car come around, then pull out again. She didn't think this could be a coincidence and felt a frisson of concern. But by the time she rushed inside, she was too tired to think. An early night sounded heavenly. If only Andre were inside waiting for her…

Over the weekend she did some research on the next case and worked on it all day Monday at the office. There'd been no sign of the new CEO. At five, Serge walked in with a strange smile and shut the door. It surprised her since he normally displayed a sterner demeanor. In his hand he held a newspaper. "You and Nicolas are a pair of dark horses. Why didn't you tell me?"

She felt that knot of panic in her stomach. It was kind of like a PTSD reaction to the unexpected after experiencing the fallout after Andre's death. "What do you mean?"

"Stop pretending, Anelise." He grinned and put the newspaper in front of her. She looked down and noticed an article on the lower half of the second page of *Paris Now*, a lowbrow, alternative afternoon paper. The headline stood out.

"New Love for One of the Bachelor Billionaire Triplets?"

Her gaze fixed on the piece that followed.

For the second time in two years, gorgeous, hunky billionaire Nicolas Causcelle is off the market! All female hopefuls will have to look elsewhere now. Insider sources report that his former fiancée, Denise Fournette, is "devastated" that Causcelle has found love again so soon after brutally casting her off. Sadly she didn't have the financial means to make the grade for a Causcelle.

His new lover is reputed to be media-shy Anelise Lavigny, only child and daughter of multimillionaire Hugo Lavigny. In this case it took money to capture money. Mademoiselle Lavigny was said to be "inconsolable" after losing her engineer fiancé Andre Navarre in a car crash only nineteen months ago, but this liaison between two of France's biggest commercial dynasties seems to have soothed her pain. Who says money doesn't talk?

The Causcelle triplets have long been the target of scheming mamas. Although since one of them seems to have disappeared off the face of the earth, that leaves only two delicious men to snap up. Good luck, Mademoiselle Lavigny. One has to wonder if the golden boy has staying power this time, or if he'll cast you away in the end.

Anelise read the article twice while the scorching heat of fury crept through her entire body. She took a deep breath and shot to her feet, handing the paper back to Serge, who was waiting for a response with a gleam in his eyes. "Someone must hate Monsieur Causcelle or me so much they were willing to risk a slander suit in order to get this lie printed for the whole world to read."

The gleam disappeared. "I'm very sorry."

"So am I. Is Monsieur Causcelle in?"

"He's on a conference call."

"I'm leaving now. Will you tell him I wish to talk to him when he *is* available? This is my cell phone number."

"Bien sur."

The moment he was gone, she pulled her purse out of the drawer and left the building, sizzling with the kind of rage she'd never known before.

Anelise had been forced to live with the intrusion of the media for weeks after Andre's death. She'd tried to hide away in order to grieve in private. But being an heiress had made her fodder for the press. The coverage dwelled on her financial assets and made a mockery out of the most painful experience of her life. To bring Andre's name into this article and hurt his family again was unconscionable.

As for the article about Nic Causcelle, it was a major hit piece that had done more damage than a nuclear bomb. Not only was the lie about the two of them horrific, but to expose his former fiancée, and allude to their missing brother was criminal! Both her life and his had been served up to the public like a feast on which millions of people would gorge.

You could print a denial, but no one would care or believe it. By ten tonight the news about the two of them would be all anyone talked about. She refused to stand for it!

She hurried inside her suite and tossed her suit jacket on the couch. The whole thing was so ugly, there was only one thing to do. Anelise would resign immediately and move to Orleans, where she could get an attorney position with the company owned by her mother's family. They manufactured foods and beverages under the name Sabayon et Fils. Living there she would be out of the limelight and could visit her parents on weekends via the A10. It was only an hour-and-a-half drive.

Before she did anything else, she phoned Serge. Forced to leave a message, she said, "I can't work for the Causcelle Corporation a second longer. You know why. I'll turn in my resignation to Monsieur Causcelle, of course. I just wanted you to know I'm making arrangements to leave Paris. Thank you for all you've done for me."

For the next hour she packed her bags, gathered her belongings and took everything out to her car. She'd drive to Orleans tonight in case reporters had already camped on her parents' doorstep waiting for sight of her.

Thankfully the author of the slanderous announcement hadn't mentioned her connection to her mother's family and their business interests. Anelise ought to be safe. *For now anyway...*

En route she phoned her parents and told them what had happened. She planned to stay at a bed-and-breakfast in Orleans where no one would know her. At least not for the moment.

"It hasn't been on the news yet."

"Wait till the ten o'clock news, Papa."

"Darling—you can stay with your *tante* Marie."

"No, Maman. I wouldn't do that to her. I'll be fine and will call you when I'm settled." Anelise needed privacy right now.

"Do you think this was retaliation because you won that suit?"

"I don't know."

"It sounds like someone wants revenge," her father exclaimed.

Anelise shuddered to think anyone could be that evil. "I promise I'll call you in a little while. Don't open your door to anyone. Love you."

Heavy traffic made it a two-hour drive. She ate at a drive-through and found a one-bedroom at a bed-and-breakfast where she registered under the last name Mattice, her mother's maiden name.

CHAPTER THREE

AT TEN TO 7:00 p.m., Nic ended the conference call with a Realtor who hadn't been honest with him. He intended to put Helene on the case, but she wouldn't be back in the office for several days because of a family funeral. It would keep until then.

After making a few notes on the case, he got to his feet intending to leave for the night when George buzzed him. "You received a call from Mademoiselle Fournette. She'd like you to call her when you get a chance."

Denise had called him? For the love of heaven, why? They hadn't spoken since their breakup two years ago. "Thanks for telling me."

Just then Serge appeared in the doorway. "I'm glad I caught you in time, Nicolas." The man looked flustered.

"What's wrong?"

"*This*, for one thing." He handed him a newspaper that had been tucked under his arm. "Read what's on the second page, bottom half."

Of course. More gossip about him. Was there nothing *new* anymore?

Nic opened the newspaper and spotted the article immediately. He thought he'd read everything that could be printed or put on TV about him or his brothers. But the evil, vindictive attack on three people in this article, including the reference to their missing brother and her fiancé's lethal car crash, wasn't like anything else.

This was new, all right, scraping the absolute bottom of the proverbial barrel of treacherous lies. The monstrous person who'd done this had tentacles that had reached the corrupt powers of *Paris Now*. Nic's head reared in fury.

"I'm sorry, Nicolas, but there's more. Mademoiselle Lavigny read it and has resigned. You were on that conference call earlier, so she left the office. She wants to talk to you when you're available."

He needed to catch his second wind. Denise's phone call was no longer a mystery. An epithet escaped. "Thank you, Serge." He

handed him the newspaper. "I'll call her tonight. Under the circumstances, I won't be
in tomorrow. Take care of things, will you?"

"Tres bien." Serge left the office.

One minute later Nic took off. All the way
home his mind filed through the people who
could have done something so unconscionable. As he entered his suite, Guy rang him.

"Nicolas? I thought you should know Mademoiselle Lavigny has vacated the building
for good. She left the key with me."

That woman didn't waste any time. Who
could blame her? "Thanks, Guy."

Once off the phone, it rang again. He
checked the caller ID. "Thank heaven it's
you, Raoul."

"I just got home and saw the article. This
has to be the garbage from hell."

"In more ways than one. Denise is trying
to reach me, and Anelise resigned to Serge.
Not only that, she moved out of her suite."

"I can't say I blame her. What can I do to
help?"

"That means a lot. Put out any fires that
come your way while I phone Anelise wher-
ever she is. Then I'll call you back."

"D'ac."

He put in a call and paced the floor, waiting for her to answer. It came after the third ring.

"Thank goodness it's you, Monsieur Causcelle."

He gripped his phone tighter. "I know this news has been devastating for you on several levels, Mademoiselle Lavigny."

"I'll be all right." There was no hysteria in her voice, which surprised him. "I went through this myself after Andre was killed. Money can be a curse once the press opens the floodgates. They didn't let up and couldn't think up enough hurtful things to tear me and my family apart, including Andre's. I wanted to run away and keep on running."

Coming from her background, she really did understand. He heard genuine pain in her tone, and sensed how much she'd suffered at her fiancé's death.

"It proves to me how difficult your life must be to live in the limelight, never knowing what will be thrown at you next. I'm so sorry for you and your former fiancée. The cruelty is unspeakable. I don't know how you've survived this long."

He gripped the phone tighter. "At times I'll admit it's been a horror story. Perhaps now you can see why my brother Jean-Louis opted out ten years ago."

"I *do* see. Now he's in another kind of horror story dealing with war." Her words touched him. There was more to her than he'd surmised. It brought out his protective feelings for her, which came as a surprise. "I'm glad you called so I can resign to you. Nothing else needs to be said."

"I'm afraid there is, but not over the phone. Where are you right now?"

"In Orleans."

What was in Orleans? He realized she wasn't in the mood to explain or answer questions. That was all right with him.

"Do me a favor and come back to Paris tomorrow morning. I'll meet you in the gardens at Malmaison at ten. It will give us time and privacy to talk. I'm afraid reporters are lurking everywhere."

"Isn't it full of tourists at that time?"

"Not tomorrow morning." The Causcelle Corporation contributed to the board. He would call the president and ask that it be closed until afternoon.

"I'll be there."

"Good. See you then."

After clicking off, Nic walked over to the

window and looked through the shutters. Sure enough he saw a gang of paparazzi ranged outside in the parking lot. Anelise hadn't been far off when she'd worried about reporters being everywhere, even at Malmaison.

That settled it. He knew he needed to take immediate action to remove himself—both for his own security and so the staff here could feel at ease to do their job.

He reached for his phone and called the company that did the painting at the *palais*. He spoke to the owner, Adolphe, explaining there was an emergency. Would he send out a two-man team in their van immediately and come to his suite? They should pull up at the main entrance, and the night watchman would let them in.

While he waited, he changed into jeans and a pullover. Next, he alerted the night watchman, then called to arrange for a car to be waiting for him in front of Adolphe's business.

Soon he heard the elevator door open to his foyer and the two men walked in. "Thanks for coming. Here's a bonus for both of you." He handed them each a bill worth a hundred Euros. "Which one of you is the driver?"

"I am," said the younger Frenchman.

"Good. I need to borrow your hat and your jacket. I'd like you to stay here for ten minutes, then go back outside where a taxi will be waiting to return you to Adolphe's. I'll be driving the van and your friend back to the business. Any questions?"

"*Non*, monsieur."

The driver handed over his jacket and hat, which Nic put on. Then came the keys.

"Make yourself at home." Nic looked at the other man. "Let's go."

By now it was ten to ten and dark as they left the building. The paparazzi, perched like buzzards waiting for a meal, didn't realize what was happening. They didn't catch on to the subterfuge as he and the other guy got in the van and drove to Adolphe's business. The car Nic had ordered was waiting there, with the keys under the front license plate.

Nic said good-night to the other man, who drove home in his car. Adolphe was still inside the business. Nic gave him the van keys, slipped him a two-hundred-euro bill and explained what was going on. The older man told him to use the facilities inside the next morning before leaving for Malmaison. After shaking hands, Nic went to a drive-through for food before going back to Adolphe's, where he parked around the back with the other vans.

First, he phoned Denise, who was furious and deeply hurt over the whole thing. He commiserated with her, then told her he'd find out the name of the culprit and get back to her. Next he called his brother. "Raoul? Do you think Papa knows anything yet?"

"No. I called Corinne to make sure she didn't let him watch the ten o'clock news or see the newspaper."

"I knew I could count on you. He'll hear about everything soon enough, but not to-night. It's strange. I thought he might have hired Anelise as a willing accomplice to play into his hands to get close to me. How wrong could I have been? She left town and the business so fast, I haven't caught my breath."

"What do you mean?"

"So much has gone on, I haven't had a chance to tell you anything." For the next few minutes he explained about Anelise's reaction and her resignation. "She went through hell herself with the paparazzi when her fiancé died. I can understand why she didn't even wait long enough to talk to me before resigning. I've been wracking my brain trying to figure out who was responsible for this outrageous piece of slander."

"Don't get me wrong, Nic, but is it possible she was so upset to find out Papa retired, she would do something like that? Is it possible she hopes to become CEO one day? Do you think that's why she got out of town so fast?"

Nic sucked in his breath. After hearing her pain earlier, the mere suggestion that she was after something else distressed him. "If that's true, then she's a very sick woman." *And I've lost my faith in people.*

"What about Denise? Is she so bitter that you broke off your engagement, she would go this far?"

"I don't think so. She called me a little while ago. I've never heard her so wounded and upset. I honestly don't think she had anything to do with it."

"Is there a lawsuit going on in the hotel department that has turned ugly?"

Nic ran a hand through his hair. "Not that I'm aware of."

"Well, I'm sure you'll figure it out."

"Our brother had the right idea to leave the family when he did. You know that?"

"Let's not go there, Nic. It's too painful."

"I wonder how long we'll have to wait until Claude locates him."

"Serge says he's the best," Raoul asserted. "That's good enough for me. Right now I'm more concerned with what's happened to you. Someone's gunning for you."

"You're right. Tomorrow I'm having a private meeting with Anelise out at Malmaison. Perhaps between the two of us we can come up with the name of the person who wanted to crucify me and smear the Causcelle name, and vilified two innocent women in the process."

"I'll help all I can."

"You think I don't know that? *Merci*, Raoul, but you should be in bed. I'll call you tomorrow."

After they clicked off, Nic lowered the back of the seat and closed his eyes, emotionally exhausted. Five hours later he awakened and slipped inside the building to freshen up. Knowing he wouldn't go back to sleep, he stopped at a café for coffee, then left for Rueil-Malmaison about twenty minutes away.

Soon he drove into the estate. Josephine Beauharnais had bought the land and the dilapidated manor before her second husband,

General Napoleon Bonaparte, returned from his campaign in Egypt. He'd been in a fury over the expense, but she'd used her money to restore the house and grounds. Malmaison meant "ill-fated home" in old French, dating back to the Vikings. Considering Napoleon's downfall, including his not being able to have babies with Josephine, Nic found the place well named.

As for Nic's own misfortunes, the one thing he'd learned in his life was that everything came down to money. Whether too much of it or too little, nothing else mattered and none of it brought happiness. He'd never been able to trust the women he'd been involved with. He would always have the deep-seated fear they loved his money more than him.

Like he told Raoul, their brother Jean-Louis had gotten completely away from it and all the sins greed and covetousness had spawned throughout history. Maybe it wasn't too late for Nic, who'd never felt so desolate. He wound around to the back area and saw one lone car parked.

Anelise hadn't visited Malmaison since she was fifteen years old. She remembered the black swans on the beautiful lake and the huge variety of roses. All of it originated from the inspiration of the Empress Josephine, who'd bought the château in 1799 and had created the world she'd born to in Martinique.

That visit had been a happy time for Anelise with her parents. But not *this* morning. There were no swans out and it was too early in the season for roses.

She supposed it was the isolation that prompted Monsieur Causcelle to suggest they meet here. Not knowing what to expect, she'd parked near the entrance. Once she'd officially resigned to him, it would be over.

A darkening sky meant there could be rain within a few hours. The elements matched her state of mind. She felt a horrifying emptiness inside. It frightened her to get this down after what she'd gone through losing Andre. The old adage that you could choose to be happy or unhappy had no meaning for her on this cool May morning. She couldn't bear the thought of losing her sanity again because the media was after her over the situation now. Maybe she'd just disappear.

A tap on the rear window jerked her out of her torturous thoughts and she turned around to see a tall man through the glass, his black hair disheveled. He wore a navy blue crew neck sweater and jeans, with a slight shadow on his jaw. At first glance she had a hard time believing it was Nicolas Causcelle. On Friday, the only time she'd ever seen him, he'd been dressed in a suit and clean shaven. She put down her window at his approach.

"I see you're an early bird like me and I appreciate it," he murmured in a deep voice. With shuttered dark eyes, he looked as if he hadn't slept for a long time. But it didn't take away from his unmatchable male potency.

"Only after being attacked in the news."

"It was an attack all right. That's what we need to talk about. Shall we walk over to the lake?"

Anelise swung her jean-clad legs around and got out. He had to be six-three. In her high heels at work, she hadn't noticed the difference in their height. But in leather sandals, her five-foot-six frame felt petite by comparison. They walked toward the water.

"When I talked it over with my parents, my father felt that the hideous piece in the paper announcing Andre's death all over again was an evil act of revenge."

He nodded. "I *know* it was, otherwise you

and my former fiancée wouldn't have been mentioned."

"Agreed." She made sure her hair clip was in place, then eased her peach-colored sweater down lower on her hips. "Still, no matter how cruel the intention, you and I both have the satisfaction of knowing one thing."

"What's that?"

"The culprit willing to go to the press to humiliate you has to be living in a world of hurt neither of us can imagine."

He looked down at her. "That's a kind way of putting a malicious action."

"I've given it a lot of thought. No one would do something like that unless they were beyond desperate for your attention." She stared up into those cold bleak pools. "Do you know anyone fitting that description?"

"Millions of people and I know why."

She laughed softly, knowing it had been a foolish question. "Do you have a way of finding out who influenced *Paris Now* to print it?"

"I could, but I'd rather discover the source with your help. You found the problem in the merger at court last week and won the case.

With your intelligence, it's possible we'll figure out the name of this wretched soul."

They walked along, listening to the birdsong in the trees. "Has this ever happened to you before?"

One dark brow quirked. "Raoul and I are in the news constantly, but this is something new."

"In other words, the article was personally vindictive in the most destructive way imaginable."

"*Exactement*, just like it was for you."

Anelise finally dared to say what was on her mind, but couldn't meet his eyes. "Forgive me if this seems impertinent, but it sounds like a woman. Have you been seeing someone who *wants* to be all important to you?"

He stopped walking. "If there were such a person, I would have dealt with her already."

She turned to him. "Since your father hired me, do you think another woman wanted the position I was given in order to get close to you?"

He rubbed his jaw. "I'm sure there are many female attorneys who'd like to work for us. But since I wasn't even a consideration as head of the hotel department when Papa offered you the job, that scenario doesn't fit."

Thoughts were firing in her mind. "Was your former fiancée an attorney?"

"No. Denise was a well-brought-up young woman of Parisian society my father felt would make me an excellent wife. I'll answer your next question before you ask it. Neither of us were in love, but I liked her better than any woman I'd met and thought we could make a go of it. It didn't work and she had an affair.

"That woke me up and I refused to go through life living a lie, not when both of us needed something more. So, I broke off the engagement. It was an amicable separation, but my father wasn't happy about it."

"Of course not. Has she seen the article?"

"Yes. We've talked about it and I'm convinced she wasn't the one who planted the story. Otherwise, she would never have gotten involved with another man in the first place. She needs to find happiness."

"So do you."

"We all do." Then she heard a sigh. "I'm afraid happiness is an elusive quality."

His lonely comment got to her. "I was happy with Andre. Truthfully, I can't imagine living with a man I couldn't love heart and soul, or who couldn't love me the same way."

He studied her face with new intensity. "Yours was a true love affair."

"Yes. Andre was my whole life."

"I'm sorry that happened."

So am I. "But it did." She smiled at him, wanting desperately to put the sadness behind her. "What I don't understand is why this person linked *my* name with you."

He cocked his dark head. "Do *you* have an enemy? Someone at your law school who was jealous of you? Serge said you were top in your class. He was very impressed."

"That's propaganda," she scoffed. "I guess we could all name a person who would wish us harm, but I haven't the faintest idea who that would be."

His penetrating gaze found hers. "What about a woman who might have loved your former fiancé and lost him to you?"

Anelise shook her head. "There was no one else for either of us. After his death and my graduation from law school, I worked at my father's company for a few months. I felt I was friends with everyone in the head office. Then your father contacted me. As I understand it, no one knew about it until he offered it to me, so the position at Causcelle was never posted."

"Papa keeps his cards close to the chest. Your appointment came as a surprise to everyone."

"Monsieur Causcelle, is there—?"

"Drop the monsieur and call me Nic," he interrupted her. "Now go on. What were you going to ask?"

She shifted her weight as they stood on the gravel. "Do you think one of *your* sisters would have liked the position I was given? Perhaps even coveted it?"

He actually burst into laughter, the deep male kind. It was the first time she'd ever seen him smile or laugh. The man was incredibly appealing. "My sisters didn't study law and wouldn't be caught dead in a courtroom. They love the pastoral life too much. Papa knew it. However, when his triplets came along, he was determined to change all that. But it didn't work."

Anelise eyed him frankly. "In other words, he couldn't take the pastoral out of his boys either." There she went again, speaking her mind before thinking how it would affect him.

"If you knew Raoul, you'd see a case in point."

"Forgive me. I should never have said anything. What about your extended family? I understand your father has a brother."

"Two actually. Our *oncle* Raimond, who heads the estate in La Racineuse and plans to die on the job he loves. The other one is our *oncle* Blaise. He's a professor of Latin and Greek here in Paris and uninterested in the family business, but his married son, Pascal, works with Raoul and me. We all get along great. Pascal is our age and a big entrepreneur like Papa."

"I can see that no one in your family is out to hurt you."

"But it's not beyond the realm of possibility," he added. "Keep thinking with that razor-sharp brain of yours. Together we'll come up with the answer."

"I don't know. Do I dare ask if Serge or Helene resent me coming into the company?"

He put his hands on his hips. "Those two were handpicked by my father years ago. They would never question his decision to hire you since I understand they told him they needed another person in there."

"I see." She spotted a bench in the distance and started walking toward it.

"Let's sit down and pool our resources, Anelise. Mind if I call you that?"

"Of course not."

He sat next to her. "I know you're planning to resign, but I'd rather you didn't. For one thing my father needed another attorney and you were his choice. I want you to have the chance to build your career here. We know that attack was aimed at me and I don't want it to be the reason you leave. I say we fight this thing through and eventually the guilty party will emerge."

"How do we fight when everyone will now assume we're a couple?"

"They'll assume more than that and you know it," he asserted, "so let's turn the lie into reality. Instead of my suing the paper and ruining them and the culprit in court, it might fun to let it stand. I have a plan. What would you think if we pretend to be madly in love? When we show up at the office tomorrow as an engaged couple, we'll convince them that money has nothing to do with our intense attraction."

Her head reared. It took a minute before

her heart rate returned to some semblance of normal. "You're not serious."

A devilish smile curved a corner of his mouth, making him too gorgeous by far. "I can't think of anything more satisfying. This person who is out to destroy me won't believe their malicious joke has turned on them. You and I will be the nine-day wonder of the media and voted the most in-love pair in history."

"The press *would* print something like that." Her voice shook. "You're right. The headlines would be spectacular."

"The press will have a field day. Every article and photo of us together will plunge the dagger deeper into our adversary, making the backfire complete. During that time, we'll catch the person who thought they'd destroyed three people. When they see their ploy didn't work, they won't be able to stay quiet about it."

Anelise got up from the bench. "Your plan makes a strange kind of sense, but I need to talk this over with my parents first. If you don't mind, I'm going to drive back to Paris now and see them."

He walked her toward her car. "Call me from their home after your visit. If you decide not to go along with my plan, we'll think of another one. Let me give you my cell phone number."

She reached in her purse for her cell and he put his number in the phone. Once ensconced in the car, she looked up at him. "There's a lot to think about. I'm just afraid the paparazzi will already be installed outside my parents' home."

"It's possible, but I know you'll handle it." She took his comment as a compliment. "Thank you for meeting me here, Anelise. No matter what we decide, I feel better than I did when I drove in."

His trait of honesty could only be admired. So could his calm in the face of such a horrible situation. "I know what you mean. Expect a call from me in the next couple of hours."

A half hour later she found her parents eating lunch in their breakfast room. To her surprise and relief, their home wasn't under surveillance yet, but it wouldn't be long. That was probably because the press was still focused on Nic.

"You're back from Orleans!" her mother cried in surprise. "Just in time to enjoy a meal with us."

She sat down at the table. "I met Nic at

Malmaison earlier this morning. We've been talking everything over."

"We've been talking too," her father interjected.

"He has a plan, Papa, but I told him I wanted to run it by you first."

"I'd like to hear it." His blue eyes smiled. "If he's the genius his father is, it ought to be a good one."

"Nic doesn't want to take the newspaper to court or find the person who had that article printed and sue them. He's not only asked me to stay on with the corporation, he would like us to pretend we're an engaged couple madly in love. His theory is that it will boomerang on the culprit responsible and we'll find out who it is." She looked away. "His suggestion is as outrageous as the smear piece in the paper."

"But very clever," came her mother's unexpected comment.

Her father started to chuckle. "Your mother's right, and I have my answer. He's Louis's son all right. It's the kind of thing he would have done himself."

Her mother nodded. "Those triplets have been chased and harassed for years. Nicolas has been in the news since his breakup with his former fiancée. The press has speculated who will be next. Nic has a real point. His pretend engagement to you will kill the endless curiosity about him. In time the journalists will concentrate on his brother Raoul, poor thing."

Anelise stared at both of them. "But *I* can't pretend to be his fiancée in order to keep my job."

"Of course not, sweetheart."

"We're strangers to each other. He's a troubled man, and—"

"You're still mourning Andre's passing," her mother broke in, reaching out to pat her hand.

"My dear daughter," her father began, sitting back in the chair. "Louis asked you to come and work for him for a very important reason. I never did tell you about the beginning of our friendship three years ago. It's time you heard our story."

Anelise had always wondered and sensed this revelation was of vital importance.

"I had stopped to eat at a café on the Rue Saint-Dominique in Paris when a man ran in with a gun and killed another man at the bar."

"*What?* How awful!" she cried.

"It was. After he disappeared, probably through a back door, the police came and everyone inside was detained for questioning. Two people said they thought *I* was the man who'd fired the fatal shot, but the gun was nowhere to be found."

"I don't believe it." Anelise shook her head, astounded.

"Another man stepped forward and told the police I *wasn't* the killer. He said he'd seen the man up close and the shooter was wearing an unusual signet ring with a snake on it. I was taken to police headquarters and there was a lineup. I swore on my life that I wasn't the accused man, but I was put under house arrest."

Her mother put a hand to her heart. "I lived in agony for a week. You'll never know how awful it was."

"For me too." Her father nodded. "The man who swore I wasn't the accused man paid my exorbitant bail. A week later the killer, the member of a notorious gambling group who wore that ring, was found. And the man who stood by me was Louis Causcelle."

"*That's* how you met?" Anelise was incredulous.

He smiled. "Since that day, we've been good friends, but agreed to keep the entire incident private from everyone, even our families. Your mother was the exception. I gave him back the bail money. When I tried to give him the title to a business I had bought, he refused it. He said he didn't want a reward. But since he knew you were in law school, Anelise, he promised he would hire my daughter when you became an attorney as a form of recompense. He said he needed a brilliant one he could trust."

"I'm finally beginning to understand." Anelise's voice trailed. This was her father's unspoken plea that she go along with Nic's plan.

"Louis was such a good man and had a hard time after losing his wife," her mother interjected. "They had three daughters, and then she died giving birth to triplet boys. He's been a wonderful father. We're both proud of our children," she added. "I just hope Louis hasn't learned about that terrible article in the paper."

"I'm sure he has, Maman."

"Nothing escapes Louis," her father assured them, "but he knows his son will handle it. Otherwise, Nicolas wouldn't have been put in charge as CEO of the hotel division."

He smiled at Anelise. "However, where you're concerned, you do whatever it is you feel you have to do in order to be comfortable. You're welcome to come back to work with me, or work for your mother's family. Maybe you'd rather do something else entirely different."

Oh, Papa. For once he was transparent as glass.

"Absolutely," her mother complied. "We're here for you always."

"I know that. You're saints."

Her parents laughed, but her thoughts were on Nic. Did *he* somehow hear the story behind their fathers' close relationship? Was that why Nic had suggested he and Anelise pretend to be engaged? Because he knew his father wanted to keep the promise he'd once made to Hugo? That was something she had to find out. She wanted to remain with the corporation for her own merits.

"If you two will excuse me? I have to make a phone call." She got up from the table and went into the salon.

Do whatever it is you feel you have to do in order to be comfortable.

CHAPTER FOUR

AFTER A SHOWER in his suite, Nic was shaving when his cell rang. He reached for it and wandered into the bedroom. It was Mademoiselle Lavigny. His pulse quickened before he clicked on. "Anelise?"

"Hello, Nic." She sounded strangely quiet.

"Are you all right?"

"That's my question to you. I don't know what I am. Before anything else, I need you to be honest with me about something important."

He frowned. "I'll do my best."

"Your father and mine met three years ago and became friends. Do you know the reason why?"

Her question was the last thing he would have expected. "I've always been curious, but I have no idea."

"That's the truth?" Her question penetrated his insides.

"I don't lie, Anelise, but it's clear you've asked me that for a reason."

After a slight pause, "I just learned about it today. Your answer has helped me make the most important decision of my life to date."

He gripped the phone tighter. "Which is?"

"If you want me to go on working for you and pretend we're engaged and mad about each other, I'm willing to do it until the culprit comes out of the woodwork."

Nic's tense body relaxed at her words. "It's the answer I was hoping for, but we need to see each other in person before we talk strategy. I'll want honesty from you too. Be prepared to tell me how and why our two fathers became friends. Will you do that?"

"I promise."

"Where are you right now?"

"My parents' home."

"Since you know the way to the *palais*, Guy will show you the elevator to my suite."

"But the paparazzi—"

"Don't worry. I've doubled security on the parking lot. I also added your name to the approved list at the desk. You'll be able to get in without being challenged or accosted. How does that sound?"

"I can't ask for more than that."

"*Bon.* We'll talk over a late lunch."

"Fine. I'll be there shortly." She ended their call.

He ordered a light meal, then alerted Guy and got dressed in a sport shirt and chinos. A half hour later the same woman he'd watched drive away from Malmaison entered the foyer from the elevator.

"Thanks for getting here so quickly, Anelise. No problem in the parking area?"

"No. I saw four guards."

"Good. I didn't know until Friday night that you'd been living here for the last month. Come in the salon and make yourself comfortable."

Nic had enjoyed relationships with several women over the years, but he'd never entertained another woman in his suite, not even Denise. Though engaged, they'd maintained separate residences. He'd always needed some time alone in his life and this suite was the best place for him. Because of this latest smear article, his whole order of life had been disturbed in a brand-new way.

His only consolation for asking Anelise to

go along with his plan rested in the knowledge that she'd lost her fiancé. Her emotions were no more involved with Nic than his with hers. Their one expectation was to expose the person who'd upended their world. Once discovered, they could put the ghastly incident behind them.

"I know you're as anxious as I am to get this over with." She found a place on one end of the sofa and sat back looking relaxed as she crossed her elegant jean-clad legs.

He sat down on a chair opposite her. "Before we go any further, I'd like you to keep the promise you made to me over the phone. What you said has aroused my curiosity."

Her gaze met his. "It's a touching story about both our fathers. I know my father would never have told me anything if that article hadn't been printed." The wistfulness in her voice, the hint of tears, got to him. In the next few minutes, she'd told him everything. "Since your father knew the same mind-blowing thing could have happened to him, he did everything he could to clear my father's name."

Astounded and moved by what he'd learned, Nic got to his feet and walked around the salon.

Anelise kept talking. "Your father is a saint, with a compassion rare to most people. It's no wonder my father has felt indebted to him and wanted him for his friend. It puts everything in a new light." By now she was wiping her eyes. "Who would ever have thought that was how the two of them met."

"Not in a million years."

"To see someone shot to death, and then be blamed for it. I can't comprehend it."

Nic sucked in his breath. "I'm still trying to wrap my head around the fact that my father testified over your father's innocence and paid his bail. If he hadn't come forward—if the real killer hadn't been caught—your father might have ended up in prison!"

She nodded. "You'll never know my father's joy when your father offered me the position, Nic."

"You became the sacrificial lamb."

"I'd do it again knowing what I know now. The important thing at this stage is to prove myself to you and your father."

"You already have by winning your first case."

No one in Nic's family knew the story. Yet his father had confided his pain over Jean-Louis to Anelise because she was Hugo's daughter. Nic felt shame, not only that he'd ever believed his father would try to force him into marriage, but that Anelise would be a part of that plan.

Louis had really liked Denise and had felt she'd make Nic a wonderful wife, but Nic searched his heart and knew his father had never pressured him to marry her. Nic had allowed his hurt over the problem with their brother to think the worst about his father, but Anelise's revelation had changed everything.

"I'm profoundly grateful that you've confided this to me, Anelise. Let's go in the dining room and start planning our next move while we eat."

He'd asked the waiter from the kitchen to set things up and got no argument from Anelise. She appeared hungry too while they enjoyed a chef salad and croissants.

"Are your things still in Orleans?"

"No. I only stayed there overnight at a bed-and-breakfast. I'd planned to work for my mother's family there, but you called so I came back to Paris."

"Where are your things?"

"In my car."

"I mean furnishings."

"At my parents' home."

He lowered his coffee cup. "I've given it a lot of thought and am proposing you move into my suite until we catch this person. There's a guest room that's never been used. Just so you know, Denise and I never lived together. It will be yours. Since everyone will think the worst anyway, it will make it easy for us to walk to work every day and discuss cases. It will keep the rumor alive until we want it to die down."

"I think it's a good idea that could work." She finished her roll.

He smiled. "Let's slip down to your car right now and bring up your luggage."

"I only have two suitcases."

"Heaven," he murmured.

She laughed as they left the suite and retrieved her belongings. Once back inside, he walked her into the empty bedroom. "Behold your new home. After you've freshened up in your en suite bathroom, we'll go shopping and celebrate our engagement at the revamped Jules Verne Restaurant at the *Tour Eiffel.*"

Her head lifted. "When?"

"Tonight. What better time to nail the person who's waiting for me to retaliate?"

A smile lit up her face. "They'll never see *this* coming. Ooh, I'm glad I have my black dress with me. We know the press won't be able to contain their joy when you show up there. Give me an hour."

His dark brows lifted. "Only one? You're an amazing woman."

"Keep that thought while we get ready to convince our world audience it's a match made in heaven."

Nic chuckled and left her bedroom. Now that she'd agreed to go along with his plan, he was excited to begin the great deception. There was no time to lose. After changing into a black tuxedo, Nic phoned his brother.

"*Eh bien*, Raoul. You have no idea what has happened since the last time we talked." In the next few minutes he told him his plan. "We'll know if we've aroused curiosity when we watch the ten o'clock news tonight. I've already phoned Corinne so she won't let Papa watch it. I should be home by eleven and I'll call to tell you more. Hang on to your hat."

"I'm already planted in front of my TV."

For the next hour Nic made a dozen phone calls in order to turn this evening into front-page news that would reach across Europe.

The last call went to the manager at Causcelle's luxury cars. "Bonsoir, Pierre."

"Monsieur Causcelle? It's an honor to hear from you. How can I help? If you need today's report, I have it here."

"*Non, non.* That won't be necessary. What I need is for you to ask Rudi to bring *la voiture noire* to the *palais.*" Bugatti's latest eighteen-million-dollar design was the new rage. "Tell him to leave it and the keys with the valet. I'll need it for this special night as soon as he arrives."

"Of course, monsieur. We'll get it ready immediately. May I ask why this is such a special night, or is it a secret?"

"It won't be one for long."

"How exciting. Enjoy it!"

"*Merci*, Pierre.

Nic could have called a dealership selling the twenty-eight-million-dollar Rolls-Royce Boat Tail, but he wanted to use his family business. Even more, he knew Pierre would tell everyone in sight. The man loved cars, but gossip was his major business. Nic imagined the paparazzi would already be here to take pictures when he and Anelise walked out to get in the car. This was going to be a fun night forcing the culprit from the shadows.

When he thought about it, he realized he hadn't had this feeling of sheer fun in years.

Anelise phoned her parents to tell them what she and Nic had decided to do. Both of them approved of his plan.

After hanging up, she hurried to turn herself into an ecstatic, love-struck woman engaged to one of the famous Causcelle triplets.

Once showered, she applied makeup. A little liner for her eyes, a pink frost lipstick and some blusher. She chose to wear her pearl earrings. Next came the dress. The only one that would work was a classic black sheath with spaghetti straps. She'd bought it to wear with Andre, but he'd died before she'd had the chance.

Until now she hadn't imagined ever putting it on, but this pretend engagement provided the perfect opportunity. Tonight she was glad she'd decided to hold on to it for an important occasion. She would combine it with her strappy black high heels and small black-beaded clutch bag.

After brushing out her hair that fell to her shoulders from a side part, she sprayed on a little fragrance. At last, she felt ready and opened the bedroom door. Her heart pounded as she walked into the salon, hoping she would live up to Nic's expectation of a Causcelle fiancée.

He stood near the couch with one hand holding his phone. The coloring of his olive skin and vibrant black hair took her breath. He'd dressed in a black tuxedo and ruffled white shirt, the epitome of an unbelievably gorgeous man. A moan came out of nowhere to escape her throat. Nic must have heard it and their gazes connected. She felt him study every inch of her before hanging up.

"Forgive me," sounded his deep voice. "I've been waiting for Anelise Lavigny. Do you happen to know where she might be?"

She played along, enjoying his sense of humor. When she'd first met him, his serious demeanor had led her to believe he didn't possess one. "I think she left with a man named Nicolas Causcelle."

He moved closer to her. "You'll have to forgive me if I hardly recognize you."

"You took the words right out of my mouth."

His midnight eyes had come alive. "The only thing missing in this scenario is a diamond ring befitting your beauty. We'll take care of that after we leave here."

"I can hardly wait," she teased.

"Be aware of photojournalists watching our every move."

"I'll follow your lead."

A smile broke the corner of his compelling mouth. "Shall we go?"

They walked through the salon to the entrance hall and got in his private elevator. Anticipation for the night ahead with this unusual man left her a little breathless. But she came close to losing it altogether when they exited the *palais* and she saw a sleek black car parked outside the entrance.

If there were flashbulbs from the reporters photographing them, she never gave it a thought. Being with Nic made her feel protected. She'd lost her fear of the media. Right now her thoughts were on the ruse they were playing. She liked the idea of getting back at the press and had never been more excited.

Nic helped her in and walked around to get behind the steering wheel.

He flashed her a glance. "What do you think?"

Without conscious thought she cried, *"Holy Bugatti!"*

A round of deep male laughter poured out of him, the happiest sound she'd ever heard.

"Nic Causcelle—I think you're a new incarnation of Batman come to earth in a revolutionary Batmobile. Will we be flying to the Eiffel Tower?"

"Not quite." He still fought laughter. "We have a stop to make at ground level first."

He drove like Mario Andretti, leaving any reporters far behind in their wake. Before long they parked outside Xan, the most famous, expensive jeweler in Paris.

Anelise had seen pictures of the designer. She was an attractive blonde genius renowned for her unique collections that drew the rich and famous, kings and queens, from around the world. This was heady stuff. Anelise needed to be careful she kept her feet on the ground throughout this whole charade.

"Are you ready? This is it."

She glanced at him. "I'm dying to see what happens next."

"In your first life I think you were a private investigator."

"Maybe."

He levered himself from the driver's seat and came around for her. This time when she got out, he put his arm around her waist and ushered her inside. The elegant store had a few well-dressed customers, but the way he held her close to his hard body, she couldn't think.

Xan herself hurried over to speak to Nic and welcomed him like an old friend. "I'm honored you would come."

"I wouldn't have gone to anyone else. Xan? Please meet my fiancée, Anelise Lavigny, the love of my life." To Anelise's shock, he leaned close and kissed her on the mouth with surprising warmth, which she reciprocated. "We need a very special ring."

The woman smiled. "If you can tear yourself away from her long enough to come into my office, Nicolas, we'll figure things out."

Anelise blushed before Nic put his arm around her shoulders and followed the designer to the private office at the end of the store. She told them to sit down at the case in front of her. "After you called me, I gathered a variety of my favorites for you. Take your time looking. I'll be back. This will be the most important ring you'll ever wear." She left the room.

Nic clasped her left hand and lifted it to his lips. "What do you think? I want you to be happy."

They didn't have to pretend right now, but Nic had gotten in character and she didn't want to let him down. "All of these diamond rings leave me speechless. They're beyond my range of imagination."

She thought about the one-carat princess cut diamond ring Andre had given her. It sat in her jewel box at her parents' home. He'd picked it out ahead of time. She'd thought if she ever married one day and had a daughter, she'd give it to her.

Nic squeezed her hand a little tighter. "Which one draws your eye the most?"

"I admit there is one, but the diamond in that intricate gold setting is far too large."

Nic nodded. "It's the round solitaire set in white gold, isn't it? That one caught my attention first. I surmise it's eight carats. You have excellent taste, Anelise. Xan says the round shape brings out the most sparkle and brilliance of all the diamonds." He reached for it and slid it onto her ring finger. It actually fit!

Just then Xan came back. "Ah—you've chosen my favorite. Did you know the round shape represents eternal love? I've found over the years that those who love this cut are inwardly trustworthy, traditional and honest."

He nodded. "The ring found the right woman all right. We'll take it."

Anelise looked into those black eyes smiling at her. "Y-you mean it, Nic?" she stammered, hardly able to get the words out.

"It's made for you, *ma belle*." He kissed her with passion right in front of Xan. Once again it was impossible to judge what was real and what wasn't. Her head swam as he touched one of her pearl earrings. "These are lovely, but tonight calls for the diamond earrings in the other case. I like the clusters."

Xan pulled out the tray while Nic removed the pearls and put them in his tuxedo jacket. The touch of his hands and skin on her body had sent darts of electricity through her. Did he know what he was doing to her? The designer placed the tray in front of them.

"Let me put these on you, Anelise. These represent eight carats of diamonds to match your ring," he whispered. She tried to sit still while he adorned her ears. Xan gave her a hand mirror to look into. They sparkled through her hair and she felt transformed.

"Perfection," Xan declared with genuine charm.

"One more thing. We'd like to see that diamond pave bracelet over there," he added. Xan brought it and he fastened it on Anelise's right wrist. It was dazzling in the light, causing her to gasp.

"Stay right there you two while I take a picture for my personal portfolio."

Anelise was so mesmerized, she couldn't have moved while the designer used her phone camera to snap them. On impulse Anelise kissed Nic first to thank him, and suddenly he was responding hungrily. She knew the other woman was taking pictures of that kiss too.

Once he relinquished her mouth, he helped her up from the chair and turned to Xan. "Thank you for your invaluable help and your artistry. This is a moment we'll remember all our lives. Now we have to leave or we'll be late for our own engagement celebration."

"Your business means the world to me." She walked them to the entrance of the store.

Half a dozen members of the press taking pictures had gathered around the car parked outside along with a crowd of spectators. Nic fielded the questions with a heartbreaking smile no woman could resist. As he helped her in, he gave her a swift kiss on the lips that would be caught by every camera.

The Eiffel Tower stood 1,063 feet tall on

the Champ de Mars, not that far from the jewelry store. She noticed the seven thirty traffic moving toward it had grown heavier, but she couldn't take her eyes off the engagement ring and bracelet.

"It's hard to believe that some people can actually buy the kind of jewels I'm wearing. When I was in *ecole primaire*, we read a book that had a story about a boy who found a pile of jewels in the forest left by the fairies. Even on the page they seemed to sparkle. I kept the book and turned to that page over and over again for years, feasting my eyes on their brilliance and wishing I could handle them.

"Tonight, not a fairy but a man put sparkling jewels on my finger, wrist and ears. I know I only get to wear them for a little while, but I've been granted an old wish. When you conceived the plan to expose the culprit, I never dreamed I'd have the time of my life doing it with you."

He had to stop for a light and looked at her. "If you want to know the truth, I've never had more fun and I find it astonishing that there's a woman alive this easy to work with, let alone please."

His words found their way inside her until

they reached the parking area outside the famous monument. "It's a good thing I've already ordered dinner. From the look of the crowd gathering, we'll be lucky to make it before closing time."

"Except they wouldn't close knowing *you're* coming," she quipped. Together they made their way through people taking pictures and entered the exclusive electric elevator taking them directly to the restaurant. His strong arms went around her as they ascended, making her feel safe and cherished. *Remember this isn't real, Anelise. Don't get carried away.*

The maître d'hôtel met them the second they stepped inside. He fell all over Nic after greeting him.

"Marcel? May I introduce my beautiful fiancée, Anelise Lavigny."

"Ooh, la-la," the older man said with a twinkle in his eyes. "It's my great pleasure to meet you, Mademoiselle Lavigny." His eyes fastened on her ring. "May your union last forever."

He showed them through the room to the only table with a large floral arrangement and lighted candles. It had been centered at the window overlooking Paris. The other tables had been placed farther away to give them privacy.

Marcel moved the arrangement to one end so Nic and Anelise could see each other as they sat across from each other. "The wine steward will be right with you. Bon appétit. Let me know if there's anything you need."

"Everything looks perfect. *Merci*, Marcel."

Nic reached for her left hand and massaged her palm. "So far we've aroused the insatiable curiosity of everyone in this room including undercover journalists. By the time we finish dinner and leave, it's possible the person responsible for bringing us together will be among the diners."

"Let's hope so."

The sommelier poured the vintage wine Nic had ordered. He raised his glass and clinked the one she was holding. "To the most successful adventure of our lives."

Anelise couldn't help but smile. "May our triumph teach this person a lesson that will change their life, hopefully for the better."

"You think that's possible?" They both drank some. Over the rim of his glass, he stared at her. "I'm trying to decide what color of blue describes your eyes. In the candlelight they glow like sapphires, but in the jewelry store they reflected ultramarine."

"Mother says they're like sea glass. My father has always called them baby blues."

Nic smiled. "You *are* his baby."

She chuckled. "Your eyes are different in different lights too."

He leaned forward. "Black is black."

"Oh, no. Black is a shade, not a color, but it takes on many nuances. When I first met you, they looked a dull black like gunmetal."

"Seriously." She'd surprised him.

"Yes, as if you were worlds away. But when we sat in your office and I brought up some personal matters that I feared offended you, they turned black like India ink."

"What matters are you talking about?"

"The photograph and talk of your brother in the military."

He shook his head. "I wasn't offended, only surprised you knew so much, yet we'd never met."

"I'm truly sorry about that. Later at Malmaison your eyes didn't seem quite as stormy black. As for tonight, they're hard to describe."

"Try. I'm fascinated."

Her heart pounded in her throat. "Alive,

like the velvety fur of a black panther in the moonlight."

At this point their Chateaubriand for two with béarnaise sauce arrived, interrupting her. The filet steak melted in her mouth. Crème brûlée followed for dessert.

"This has always been my favorite from childhood," he volunteered before eating every bit of it. She saw the schoolboy in him.

"I can tell. The black of your eyes is on fire. I love this dessert too."

"Your eyes have turned an exquisite azure. In future that's the color I'll look for to know how happy you are."

She took a quick breath. "How well do you think our ruse is working so far?"

Nic finished his wine. "As far as publicity goes, we'll know a certain amount tonight when we get home and watch the ten o'clock news." He glanced at his watch. "It's recording now. The totality will be apparent tomorrow when we see the morning headlines."

To her surprise he got up from the table and pulled a white rose from the arrangement. Before she knew what was happening, he walked around to her. After kissing her shoulder, he tucked the stem of it under the spaghetti strap for everyone to see. The intimate gesture left her weak as a puddle. "Shall we go?"

Could she?

CHAPTER FIVE

ANELISE GATHERED AS much strength as she was able and got to her feet, clinging to the table until she felt stable. Nic slid his arm behind her waist and guided her across the room to the elevator. All eyes followed their progress. Some diners who must have known Nic nodded to him, but he concentrated on her.

They entered the elevator, but they might as well have been riding a meteor through the universe before reaching the ground. She'd lived in Paris all her life, but it had never appeared more magical.

Once outside the elevator she could tell the crowd of journalists and paparazzi had enlarged. With so many spectators, she couldn't see the car. Nic pulled her close and buried his face in her hair. "Is there any question we're getting more than enough splash?"

"It's so dreadful it's no wonder your brother ran for his life."

"*Dieu merci* we have an infallible method of escape."

She'd never been so thankful to reach the car. The crowd parted for them. Nic brushed her lips with his own before helping her in. After he went around to his side, he pressed the accelerator and they were off with a roar of the engine.

"Did you see the look on that journalist's face when we whizzed past him?" she cried. "I doubt he was able to get a picture until it was too late." Suddenly they both started to laugh, needing a release of tension.

Nic eyed her, his handsome face reflecting a happiness she hadn't seen until now. "He and a dozen others. What an amazing night, Anelise."

Indeed it was. The term "wined and dined" had taken on a whole new meaning she'd never forget. She turned her head to smell the sweet fragrance of the rose. He had no idea her body still throbbed from the feel of skin against skin.

When they arrived at the *palais* in record time, she blurted, "You really *were* a race car driver in another life."

His husky chuckle amused her. "Running away from the press may have made me an expert behind the wheel. But a racing career would only increase the media's coverage on me."

She nodded. "You're right. Tell me something. Even though you weren't born a singlet, what would you have pursued if you could have thrown off your business chains?"

Anelise loved it when he laughed. He unlocked the car doors. "A research scientist."

"Truly?"

"Cross my heart, but an explanation will take some time. I'll tell you upstairs later. Several cars followed us in here and now I'm tired of us being the target."

With his help she got out. As she turned, she glimpsed the back of a red car in the periphery, but it took off behind two other cars so fast, she wasn't sure of the make.

He grasped her arm and they entered the building. A younger-looking security guard she didn't recognize was on duty at the desk. "Bonsoir, Monsieur Causcelle," he said while his eyes roved over Anelise with unabashed male interest. "Congratulations on your engagement. When I came on duty a few minutes ago, Guy told me the news. I'll be covering for him for the rest of the week while he's on vacation."

"*Merci*, Robert. Give these keys to the valet and please meet my fiancée, Mademoiselle Lavigny."

"It's a pleasure, mademoiselle."

"*Enchanté*, monsieur."

After that Nic walked her down the end of the hall and around to the elevator. When the door closed, they were finally alone.

"At last," she exclaimed as they rode to the second floor. "I don't know how you've lived with this kind of attention all your life."

"That's my question for you after watching Marcel and Robert swallow you alive."

"Don't be preposterous, Nic." The elevator door opened just in time for her to escape to the salon and hide the heat creeping into her cheeks. "I'll be right back." She darted through the room to her bedroom, where she could freshen up.

After removing her shoes and hose, Anelise took off the jewelry, including the ring. She laid everything on the dresser, including the white rose, and put her watch back on. From one of the drawers, she pulled out a pewter-blue top with matching sweat pants and put them on. Once she'd run a brush through her hair, she felt ready and walked into the salon in sandals.

Nic had to be in his bedroom.

No sooner did she sit down on one of the upholstered chairs than he walked in wearing gray sweats. With his tall, rock-hard build, the man looked superb in anything. He shot her a glance. "I'm glad you got comfortable too. Would you like a sherry or a brandy? Or maybe a soda? There's cola in the fridge in the kitchen."

"Nothing, thank you, but don't let me stop you."

"I'd rather watch the news."

"I'm dying to see what came of our night out."

He found a place in the middle of the couch and reached for the remote. "We'll catch the news from other stations first, then watch the recording." A second later, the TV came on.

"This is FT-2, and now we're here at the Jules Verne Restaurant in Paris where the famous Nicolas Causcelle is dining with his new fiancée, Anelise Lavigny. Though she looks like a film star who should be on the screen, she's the new attorney for Causcelle Hotels. Imagine having her looks and a brain

as well. She graduated with top marks from the Sorbonne Law School."

As Anelise groaned, Nic turned to FT-1.

"All Paris is agog with the latest news. We're here at the Jules Verne Restaurant, where the fabulous Nicolas Causcelle has started a trend. You don't need to send your new fiancée a corsage. Simply pull a white rose out of the flower arrangement and slip it under the strap of her oh-so-becoming black dress. A match made in heaven."

Anelise would never forget that moment. "Please turn it off, Nic."

"Just one more. Let's see what's on F-3."

A video of them arriving back at the *palais* played on the screen. How did that get on the news so fast?

"And it's helpful to know they've both put their tragedies of a car crash and broken engagement behind them to find love again. We'll hope this second time around will bring them happiness. And who knows? Another set of Causcelle triplets? You can vote on-line whether they'll have three boys or three girls. No matter how long it takes, the winner will receive a new Bugatti of their choice."

She sat forward. "We're not even married,

and already there are wagers on whether we'll have triplets and what kind!"

Nic flashed her a broad smile. "Are you ready for the recording?" With a click came the familiar music of a major channel and the voice of anchor Madelaine Corot.

"Ici, Paris! Welcome to the top-of-the-hour news. No. You're not hallucinating. The man who climbed out of that sensational black Bugatti at the Tour Eiffel *is none other than gorgeous billionaire Nicolas Causcelle, one of the famous Causcelle triplets. His stunning new fiancée is Anelise Lavigny, only child and daughter of multimillionaire Hugo Lavigny. Her mother comes from the wealthy Mattice family of Sabayon et Fils Foods in Orleans. She's wearing an eight-carat diamond among other jewels as they enter the Jules Verne Restaurant. By now all eligible and not-so-eligible females have gone into mourning. Even I am still trying to catch my breath after that kiss he just gave her. Stay tuned for more and you'll understand why we're number one in the ratings!"*

"The press are impossible, Nic!"

"But tonight they did their job as never before." He shut off the TV with another satisfied smile. "Our evening turned out to be a colossal success. Now we wait for our in-furiated culprit to creep out of hiding. Since we've eliminated every possible suspect, we'll know the identity of this person right away."

She studied him for a moment. "While we've been watching, an idea came to me. Do you know who's in charge at *Paris Now*?"

"The paper is controlled by some major shareholders. Why?"

"Maybe you could ring one of them and ask them to congratulate the journalist who got the scoop on our engagement. This person might be so surprised that you're not angry over the mention of your former broken engagement in their sleazy paper, he or she will give away some vital piece of information."

Nic grinned and got to his feet. "Do you have any idea how spooky you are? I was thinking exactly the same thing while we were watching TV. There has to be some kind of radar connecting our thought processes."

"Or maybe someone above is on our side."

His black brows furrowed for the first time all night. "Like whom?"

"Your mother? She never got to raise you.

It's possible she's looking over you, watching out for your welfare now that your father is ill."

"You think?" His disbelieving tone told her not to tread further, but she couldn't help it.

"Where was your mother born? I've been wanting to ask."

"La Racineuse," he muttered.

"I had no idea. I thought she must be another Marie Curie in the making."

"Non, non." He chuckled. "Delphine Ronfleur came from a farming family too."

"I should have guessed as much. She left her imprint on all of her children, even the last three she didn't get the chance to hold and love. Tell me more about your desire to be a research scientist. Where did that come from? What kind?"

"I used to think about the cheese we made, why it was so good people would keep buying it. Everyone said it was the milk from the cows. Why *those* cows? There had to be a reason, and research would help me understand."

"That's why you seemed to know so much about the cows. Didn't you tell your father about your interest?"

He lowered his head. "*Non.* Papa always said he needed his sons to help him run the business. We didn't fight him. After high school we were sent to business college in Paris and were hounded by the press morning and night. Jean-Louis suffered the most. He loved mechanics. Before we left La Racineuse, he could repair every car, truck and farm machine on the property."

"Anyone who can repair machinery is a genius to me."

"*He* was! The guy loved working with his hands, but his college grades suffered. At that point he and Papa had bad fights. One day he announced he was leaving to go in the military. It sent our father into shock. Our family was never the same after that."

"How awful for all of you." She groaned.

"When I saw what it did to our father, I gave up my dream of science."

She looked at Nic through the mist. "What dream did your brother Raoul have to let go of?"

"Raising cattle and sheep. He spent a lot of time helping out in the pasture on our property. One time he told me David had it made being a shepherd before he slew Goliath."

"Obviously he meant it."

"There was never a question of that."

Just then Nic's cell phone rang. He took one glance. "It's Raoul. I promised him I'd call at eleven."

She checked her watch. "It's after that now. Please go ahead and return it."

"In a minute. We haven't discussed our plans for tomorrow. What I'd like to do is visit my father with you. Do you mind if we leave here at eight thirty in the morning? Pack what you need. I don't expect us to return before Thursday. I'll ask the kitchen to send up our breakfast first, then we'll leave for the airport."

His request surprised her, but she'd love to see Louis again. Right now she wanted to do whatever Nic asked until this was resolved. "I'll be ready."

"Be sure to put that ring back on."

"I will. *Bonne nuit.*" She hurried to her bedroom with so much to think about she'd be awake for hours. Tomorrow she'd find a book so she could press the rose. That had been a moment in time she'd never ever forget.

Nic turned out lights and walked to his bedroom before phoning Raoul. "I promised to call you, but the night got away from me."

"So I gathered after I saw you slip the stem of that rose under the strap of a certain black dress worn by one breathtaking woman. I took half a dozen swallows. So did any man watching and wishing they were in your place…"

He chuckled. "Cut it out. What else did you see?"

"Everything showing on the other stations. One did an interview with Xan, the designer. She flashed a picture of you kissing Anelise in a passionate embrace. It was supposed to show her new eight-carat diamond ring, but no one with hormones was paying attention."

"Give it up, Raoul."

"I'm not kidding and I'm not sure that you haven't escalated the press's interest in the two of you. I thought you wanted to get them off your back. It's better than the stuff TV has to offer. Any ideas on who did this to you?"

"Not yet."

"I don't hear you complaining in any way, shape or form if you follow my meaning. In the morning I think you'd better let Papa in on what you're doing. He always reads the *Figaro* with his first cup of coffee. There'll be headlines in every newspaper across France."

"I know. He'll be awake by six thirty. Anelise and I will fly there in the morning and stay overnight. I'll ask Corinne to get him ready for our visit. Raoul—before we hang up, I have something amazing to tell you. It puts a whole new complexion on everything."

"Even *you*."

"What do you mean?"

"There's a change in you, *mon frere*."

"Anelise revealed a secret to me no one in our family ever knew. It has taken away my negative feelings toward *Papa*."

"That sounds pretty miraculous."

"It is. There's a very specific reason our father hired Anelise and you won't believe why."

"Don't keep me hanging."

In the next breath, Nic told him everything. After hearing the revelation, Raoul blurted, *"Sainte Marie!"*

"My sentiments exactly."

"Our father kept hers out of prison!"

Nic clutched the phone tighter. "Anelise called Papa a saint. She praised him for raising us without Maman. I feel guilty over the years I've resented him for making us work in the business, and for his treatment of Jean-Louis."

"It baffles me that we never did know he suffered over losing him. Let's face it, we owe her a great deal for confiding in you."

"Agreed. Now you can see that if I had accepted Anelise's resignation, it would hurt him when what he wanted more than anything was to keep his promise to Hugo."

"It's all making sense, Nic."

"I also need to forgive Papa for trying to keep the business alive through us. He *did* need help, and he's no different than millions of other fathers."

"If you and I had deserted Papa and done our own thing like Jean-Louis, I don't want to think what could have happened to him."

Nic sank down on the side of the bed. "Neither do I. Anelise has been teaching me about forgiveness."

"What do you mean?"

"She feels sorry for the person who had that article printed in the newspaper. She doesn't see evil. It's her belief that person is in a world of pain deep down."

"Anelise could be right. She sounds like an extraordinary person."

"I believe she is, and the revelation about our father's suffering won't leave me alone."

"I know *I* haven't been easy on him for my own reasons," Raoul murmured, sounding far away.

"A lot of suffering has gone on, but right now we've got to find Jean-Louis and bring him home before it's too late for a reconciliation with Papa."

"I'll call Claude Giraud tomorrow and find out if he's learned anything."

"Let's keep in close touch."

They hung up and Nic got to his feet. Thinking about tomorrow, he phoned the office and left a message for George. Neither he nor Anelise would be in until Friday.

Before he got in bed, he called the Causcelle pilot and arranged for the private jet to be ready in the morning. They were flying to Chalon Champforgeuil. From there they'd drive to the château to see his father. After hearing Raoul's morose tone just now, Nic had more than one mission to accomplish there. A private one...

Six hours later he showered, shaved and dressed in a business suit and tie, the kind his father liked him to wear. Louis expected his sons to look professional rather than casual. Before Nic did anything else, he phoned Pierre's office and left a message for Rudi to come for the Bugatti. Since it had done its job, Nic wouldn't need to drive it again.

A waiter from the kitchen had delivered their breakfast and the morning paper. He sat down at the table to read while he waited for Anelise.

The first page showed a photo of him and Anelise riding up the *Tour Eiffel* with his arms around her. The headline read "Billionaire Nicolas Causcelle Captures an Exclusive Market." The accompanying paragraph continued on the quarter top half of the second page with another photo. This one showed him kissing the palm of her hand across the table at the restaurant. The caption beneath made him laugh.

"I'm glad you've found something amusing in the paper." A stunning Anelise had come into the dining room dressed in a light gray two-piece business suit with a strand of pearls around her neck. She sat down before he could help her and reached for the coffee he'd poured. "But I'm afraid to ask why."

"There's a photo of us in the restaurant." He handed her the paper, pleased she'd left her dark blond hair loose. Like silk.

Her head lifted and her gaze met his with a smile. "*Besotted?* Is that word even in use anymore?"

"It is now, and we're stuck with it." He chuckled while they ate their eggs and brioche in no time. "Are you packed?" Nic was excited to get going. He would be seeing his father again, this time through *new* eyes.

"My overnight bag is in the salon."

"Then I'll grab it and we'll head downstairs. I've sent for a limo to take us to the airport. I'm anxious to make sure the Bugatti has been picked up. First, however, I need to return these."

He reached in his pocket and handed her the pearl earrings he'd removed last night. "They'll match the necklace you're wearing."

"I was going to ask you for them. Thank you for remembering, Nic." She put them on.

"A gift from the man you'd planned to marry?" He knew next to nothing about her former fiancé.

She averted her eyes. "No. The necklace and earrings belonged to my grandmother on my mother's side."

"You look lovely in them. The ring looks great on you too," he said before leaving the table to get her overnight bag. He'd put his bag in the foyer. Once downstairs they walked down the hall and around to the entrance.

Robert stood to greet them. "Bonjour, Monsieur Causcelle, Mademoiselle Lavigny. Your limo is waiting."

"*Merci*, Robert. *Ça-va?*"

"I'm all right now that the Bugatti has been picked up. A lot of people have driven in and out of the private parking area all night. They would get out to take pictures and try to come in asking questions about you and your fiancée. The guards told them to leave the premises or they'd call the police."

"Well, it won't happen anymore. Thanks for doing your job."

"There was one huffy driver who told the guard she was a personal friend of yours and would wait here at the desk. He told her she couldn't stay and would have to move on. She got nasty with him, but finally left."

That set off an alarm bell inside Nic. But it was Anelise who asked, "What kind of car was she driving?"

"A red Bugatti."

"I've seen it around here before."

Nic looked at Anelise as pure truth flowed through both of them. He turned to Robert.

"You all did the right thing and deserve a bonus. If she bothers the guards again, phone Raoul. He'll take care of it. We'll be back on Thursday. Hold the fort."

Robert grinned. "*Bien sur*, monsieur."

In another minute they reached the limo and climbed in the back with their overnight bags. Nic told the driver to take them to the small airport, then he looked at her. "You figured out the name of our culprit at the same time I did."

Anelise nodded. "Babette Lafrenière, the *vedette* from TV."

"That's the one. How do *you* know her?" He couldn't help but be intrigued.

"I don't, but I ran into her twice. Once in the reception area of the *palais* last Friday after court. And then in George's office later that same day after meeting you."

"The pieces are fitting together. Tell me everything."

She laughed. "Just now when Robert explained that the woman in the red Bugatti got nasty with the guard, I knew it was the same one who'd bothered Guy. I had just walked in from being at court and could hear loud voices. Guy looked totally frustrated. They were arguing about something. He called my name and told me to phone my dad. I nodded and kept walking to my apartment.

"Before I reached the door, she caught up to me using my name and said, 'I take it you live here.' When I said yes, she demanded to know how I had accomplished it. When I told her I didn't understand what she meant, she got angry and said, 'In other words, you won't tell me.'

"I explained that I didn't know what she wanted. She snapped back at me with, 'A suite, of course, but the man at the front desk is no help.'"

Nic chuckled. "I wish I could see your exchange on video. I bet her meltdown outdid any performance."

"I'm sure it did. I told her it wasn't a hotel. She would have to talk to the head of the Causcelle Corporation. With eyes blazing, she asked if that was what *I* had done. Then she said in a patronizing tone, 'Isn't he as old and impossible as Methuselah?' All I said was, 'He's a wonderful man,' and I excused myself to go inside.

"A few hours later I went back to work where you and I met. After I left your office, I walked past George to say good-night and discovered her standing there. She looked stunned when she saw me and asked in a haughty voice what I was doing there. I've never known such rudeness.

"George hurriedly introduced me as one of the corporate attorneys. You should have seen the shock on her face. 'You're an attorney?' she cried.

"I tried to make a joke out of it and said it surprised me too." Nic burst into laughter.

"George promptly informed me I could see Mademoiselle Lafrenière on the *Paris Noir* TV series. I told her I thought that must be exciting, but I said I didn't watch much television and needed to leave for another appointment. I felt her staring daggers at me as I walked out the door. Not until I got outside did I realize how rude that must have sounded to her."

"You delivered the coup de grâce." Nic squeezed her hand that wore the diamond ring before he let it go.

She glanced at him. "How do *you* know her?"

"Over a month ago I was at our central car dealership on business. She happened to be there looking at the red Bugatti. Pierre, the manager, was working with her and introduced her to me. From that moment on she—"

"Forgot all about Pierre," Anelise interrupted, "and latched onto you. No doubt she wanted you to take her for the ride of her life and had it all planned out."

He sucked in his breath. "It didn't happen. Like you, I excused myself and left for La Racineuse. To my chagrin she found out where I lived, probably through Pierre, who talks too much. When I got back last Friday, Guy told me she'd been coming around the *palais* in hopes of seeing me. She'd kept calling nonstop to find out when I'd be back. I told him I'd take care of it."

"That explains why I saw her parked outside over last weekend," Anelise theorized. "I believe she even followed me to my parents' home on Friday."

Nic moaned. "Friday was a day to remember for a lot of reasons. Guy gave me her number and I called her when I went back to my suite. To make a short story even shorter, she asked *me* out for drinks. I told her I couldn't because I was permanently involved with another woman. That was something she couldn't fight."

"That was *your* coup de grâce, Nic."

"Or so I thought. Little did I know I'd uttered a prophecy about you and me without realizing it."

"What did she say?"

"Her comeback is imprinted in my mind. She said, 'It wouldn't be you've gone back to your former fiancée after all this time, would it? Or is this woman the formidable young attorney at Causcelle Headquarters who has brought you to your knees?'"

"The *what*?" Anelise cried.

"An interesting choice of words don't you think? I couldn't figure out how she even knew you. I told her I hoped she was enjoying her new car and wished her luck in her career."

Anelise let out a deep sigh. "Now that we know the truth, I want to learn a lot more about her. I packed my laptop. While we're in flight we'll do some research on her and see if we can find something helpful on her."

"Good idea. When we return to Paris, I'll contact Claude, the secret service agent who is doing another job for us because of what you told me. He'll help us get to the bottom of it."

CHAPTER SIX

"WHAT DID I SAY?"

"The revelation about my father's sadness over Jean-Louis couldn't have surprised me more. After I told Raoul, we both agreed we needed to find our brother and bring him home before it was too late for the two of them."

Again Nic grasped her hand, enfolding it. Though surprised, she didn't mind. Not at all. "You'll never know how grateful we are that you shared that with me. You're a wonder, Anelise."

She swallowed hard, deeply affected by his words and the way he looked at her as if delving into her soul. "I know it would thrill your father to see him again."

He nodded his dark head. "I'm counting on Claude digging up more information on Mademoiselle Lafrenière. I have to admit

I'm curious why she has picked me out of all people to ruin."

Anelise rolled her eyes. "Aside from the obvious that she's attracted to you, I'm more concerned there's an ulterior reason for why she did this to you. She might be a real danger. That's got me worried."

"Don't worry too much. Not while we're home at La Racineuse."

Home. In his heart, she knew he'd never left.

Once on board the Learjet, she opened her laptop. Nic leaned closer to see the screen and she breathed in the scent of his shampoo. If she wasn't careful, she would lose her concentration around him. In a second, she'd looked up the social media sites to find something on Babette.

"Here's a Twitter account. Two hundred followers, Nic."

"I see she'll need a lot more to catch up to Juliette Binoche's millions of fans."

"It says here Juliette has been in sixty films. I'll look up more information on Babette." With a click, a picture of her appeared above a tiny article. "Elizabeth 'Babette' Lafrenière, twenty-four, a French-Canadian performer in the television series *Chaos*.

She's single, and born in Quebec, Canada. No awards.'"

"French-Canadian?" Nic murmured. "She doesn't speak Quebecois."

"Maybe her family moved to Paris when she was a child and she lost her accent."

He shook his head. "There's no information here to help us, nothing that sounds an alarm. I'll definitely ask Claude to investigate her background."

She turned off her computer. "Before we reach your home, tell me a little about your sisters. Do they all live at the château?"

"No. Anne and Yvette have their own homes with their families on Causcelle property. The eldest, Corinne, along with her husband, Gaston, and their children, Brigitte and Honore, have moved into the château from their home to take care of Papa. We've also hired a health care nurse, Luca Rives. However, my sisters come in to help and stay when Corinne needs a break. Raoul and I have already taken turns and will come when we can to relieve everyone."

"You have a wonderful family, Nic. Everyone should be so fortunate."

"You're right. This evening you'll have the

chance to meet them at dinner. Tomorrow I'll show you around the property."

She glanced at him. "Will I see the cows that make the Causcelle cheese?"

"That's part of the plan."

"What's the other part?"

"I want to show you something that I'm thinking of turning into a business investment. You can help me decide if it's worth it."

"Now you've really intrigued me. Your eyes have the sheen of that panther I told you about last night." His male beauty had no equal.

"I'd better start wearing sunglasses."

"It's too late for that."

The fasten-seat-belts sign flashed.

A half hour later Corinne and her husband, Gaston Leclerc, met them at the entrance. After Nic hugged both of them, Anelise heard his attractive brunette sister murmur that their father had seen the news about the engagement in the morning paper.

"I thought as much." He walked Anelise through the exquisite entrance hall to the drawing room. The seventeenth-century Causcelle château contained ceilings painted to reflect its history. What a glorious home! Louis had raised his family here.

When he'd sent his boys to business school in Paris, they'd been installed at the *palais*. They'd gone from one luxurious château to a modernized palace. Each son had his own suite, but Anelise knew it pained Nic that Jean-Louis's empty bedroom was still waiting for him here.

While she studied some tapestries on the walls, a balding Louis was wheeled in the room by his caregiver, Luca. Corinne introduced Luca to her. Louis, who'd given his bone structure and handsome looks to his sons, was impeccably dressed in a suit and tie as always. He looked well cared for, but his coloring and gaunt features told her he was failing.

"The guest bedroom is at the top of the stairs on the right, mademoiselle. You can freshen up there whenever you wish." At that point she and her husband left the room with Luca to give them time alone.

Anelise smiled at Louis and walked over to kiss his cheek. "When you hired me, I never dreamed I'd be seeing you in the surroundings where you were born. It's a thrill to be in your beautiful home, Louis."

He smiled back and reached for her left hand to look at the diamond ring. "I retired just in time and am pleased Nicolas had the good sense to snap you up before some other man did. Please—sit down."

Shaken by the comment when she knew Louis had no knowledge of why she was wearing the ring, she found a seat on a damask love seat near him. Nic leaned over to kiss his father. Suddenly she saw him hug him in a gesture she knew must have surprised Louis. "It's good to see you, Papa. You look well," he said in a voice full of emotion. Then he turned to sit next to Anelise.

Her pulse raced when he unconsciously enveloped her hand in his. She knew Nic wasn't acting right now. Raw emotions caused him to reach for her. He leaned forward. "Corinne told me you saw the announcement about our engagement in the *Figaro* this morning. We came as soon as we could to explain."

Louis gazed at Nic. "You're my son, all right. You knew what you wanted the moment you saw Anelise. That doesn't surprise me. Do you know I had my eye on your mother when I was seventeen years old? We were out in the pasture in the rain. I'd only met her the weekend before. Right then I told her she couldn't marry anyone else because she belonged to me."

Anelise let out a cry of delight.

"I had bought her an engagement ring with my savings. It was a simple band, not a diamond like the one Nicolas gave you, Anelise, but it did the trick. I put it on her finger a week later, and that was it!"

"Oh, Louis—" Anelise jumped up from the love seat to give him a quick hug. "How sweet and romantic."

Nic got to his feet. "I never knew that story, Papa. Unfortunately, I can't say our story is anything like yours. Our engagement is the result of *this*!" Anelise watched him pull a news clipping from his suit pocket. "Read the article, Papa. It appeared in *Paris Now* the other day."

Louis adjusted his bifocals to look at it. "Ah… *This* is why Corinne told me the newsboy hadn't come by yet."

"The second I read it, I phoned Anelise to meet me at Malmaison to talk it over."

"And you came up with the pretend engagement idea," his father blurted. "I would have done the same thing. Smoke out the culprit. The two photographs of you in the local paper here had me totally convinced you were in love. Well done, *mon fils*. The idiot who did this will come to no good in the end."

"Anelise believes this person is suffering more than we know," Nic confided, to her surprise.

"Of course they are! Have you figured out who it is?"

They both stared at each other before saying yes.

Louis chuckled. "If I don't miss my guess, it's a woman."

"No one is smarter than you, Papa."

"That's the first time you've ever said that to me, Nicolas."

The way Nic struggled to find the right words, Anelise knew he had past regrets and was in pain.

"Over the years I've left many things unsaid, Papa. I'm ashamed of that now."

This moment had turned into something too private. Father and son deserved time alone.

Anelise slipped out of the room to the foyer. The beautiful day compelled her to walk outside in the sunlight and wander around the grounds.

With each step, Nic's words to his father

rang in her ears. *Unfortunately, I can't say our story is anything like yours.*

No, it wasn't.

Why did she feel so hurt? How could she feel anything when her world had come to an end with Andre's death?

Over the next hour she explored, but the farther she got away from the château, the more she realized a truth that shook her to the core. For nineteen months now she'd mourned Andre. Yet except for one moment, Andre hadn't been on her mind since Nic had swept into her life last Friday.

"Anelise?"

Surprised to hear Nic's voice, she wheeled around in time to see him running toward her. The sight of him caused her heart to thud, proving beyond any doubt that something earthshaking was happening to her.

He raced up to her and gripped her upper arms, breathing fast. She thought he was going to kiss her. *And she wanted him to.* "I'm sorry I was so long."

"Don't be," she begged him, trying to catch her own breath. "I know how important today is to both of you."

This time his black eyes blazed with light. "We discussed everything and made our peace. I told him we're going to find Jean-Louis and bring him home."

"I hope it's soon."

"So do I. He now knows it was Babette Lafrenière who started all the trouble. He said he was grateful to her. To quote Papa, 'She's the reason we're back to being father and son in the truest sense of the word.' Only more good can come out of this."

Her eyes smarted. Louis was a marvel. "As we've both acknowledged, your father is an exceptional human being."

Nic rubbed his hands down her arms before letting her go. It left her bereft and his touch had caused her to tremble. "He thinks you're an angel for going along with my plan, Anelise. More than anything he wants you to stay with us."

"You can tell him I want to stay because it's an honor for me. But only if it's what *you* want."

"If *I* want—are you teasing me? Don't you know you're the greatest thing that has happened to the Causcelle family?"

But what about you personally, Nic? With that question she realized she had lost her heart to him.

"I want you to look at the property I'd like

to buy. First, we'll stop at a deli for a snack along the way."

"How far is it?"

"Only two miles from here. Let's walk around to the garage for the car."

"Why is acquiring it so important to you?"

"Not for me. For my father. It's been his heartfelt wish for three decades. If I could do this for him, it would mean everything to me. I'm counting on you being my good luck charm."

Good luck charm?

She'd like to be that for Nic, but when she looked down at the diamond on her finger, more longings welled up inside her. If this kept happening, she was in real trouble because these new feelings had everything to do with Nic, not Andre.

Nic drove them to the next little village and hurried into a store for some sandwiches and coffee. They were both hungry. When he got back in the car, Nic ate before leaving for the site while Anelise nibbled her sandwich more slowly as they drove through the countryside.

Anelise looked around. "Do you know after living in Paris, the pastoral setting and cows make me feel like I've landed in a perfect universe?"

"Now you know why my brother and I love to come out here whenever we can."

Within a minute they reached the other side of the hamlet where the remains of a burned-down church came into view. Nic pulled to the side of the road.

She turned to him. "Why did you stop here?"

"*This* is the property."

"I don't understand. Fire has destroyed it. When did it happen?"

"A year after my brothers and I were born."

"But there's been no war here."

"You're wrong, Anelise." His deep voice grated. "An ongoing war of a different kind has been raging in this region for a long time. Every so often violence erupts."

Anelise knew there was a lot more to his explanation than that. "You look so troubled. Can you tell me about it?"

Nic finished his coffee. "Twelve monks were living in this monastery at the time. Eight new priests had joined them the night before the place was set on fire. No one survived and no one was caught."

Anelise came close to choking on her food. "How ghastly—"

"My uncle Gregoire, a new priest and my mother's favorite brother, had just joined them the day before the tragic immolation occurred."

"Oh, no, Nic—" Tears rolled down her cheeks.

"*Dieu merci*, my mother had already gone to heaven the year before it happened. But Papa and Gregoire had been good friends. My father never got over it. Over the years he'd hoped the place would be rebuilt and he was willing to give money in Gregoire's memory, but nothing has been done about it for fear of more retaliation. He carries that sorrow as well as the loss of my mother."

She wiped her eyes with one of the napkins. "It only takes one person who's out of his mind to destroy the lives of others. I can't fathom such cruelty…"

He inhaled sharply. "I've thought about it for a long time. What I'd like to do is buy the property for my father and turn it into a hospital/hotel in Gregoire's memory. A person would go in for surgery, and a family member would get a room to be near to him or her during their convalescence. It would be free to anyone who needed help. I mean *anyone*! No restrictions.

"I would also have the chapel recon-structed for anyone who wanted a place to pray. In fact I'm thinking of buying a few other properties around France and doing the same thing."

What had Louis told her? He knew that one day his three sons would raise the corpo-ration to new heights. A lump lodged in her throat. "That's beyond inspirational, Nic."

"It's been done in many places. But I'm afraid my proposal will get turned down over the same fear of retaliation. So what would you think if my plan included a research cen-ter as well?"

Research, the heart of Nic's dream. "Go on. I want to hear it all."

"I'm no scientist, but I do know that con-trolling disease due to pathogens that move between animals and humans has been chal-lenging. Those pathogens have been respon-sible for the majority of new human disease threats everywhere, and a number of recent international epidemics.

"Currently, our surveillance systems often lack the ability to monitor the human-animal interface for emergent pathogens. Identifying and ultimately addressing cross-species infections will require a new approach. Those resources are hard to come by."

He knew all this while running the massive Causcelle hotel network? "You mean impossible except for someone like you. I think it's the most wonderful idea I've ever heard." Anelise understood exactly what he was saying. The depths to this man left her close to speechless. "It's a genius idea that only someone of your brilliance and generosity would even consider."

He stared hard at her. "Yet you still think it will be impossible to convince the owner to sell?"

"No, Nic. After what you've just told me, I believe anything is possible. Where do you need to go to make your proposal?"

"Back to La Racineuse to talk to the archbishop of the region."

"Then let's try to arrange a meeting before we have to return to Paris."

The lines in his handsome face relaxed. "I doubt he'll be available, but hopefully the bishop will agree to give us some time today. With my scholarly attorney to support me, why not?"

Yes, she *was* a Causcelle attorney, but

no scholar. She wished she didn't want to be anything more to him. Since their engagement, she feared that this pretense had started to become reality for her. Yet she knew their fake alliance was only temporary in Nic's mind.

His prophetic words came to fruition when they reached the church and he was told the archbishop was away on business. She felt Nic's disappointment. The secretary showed them into the office of the bishop, who greeted Nic warmly, and introductions were made.

Anelise listened while Nic explained his purpose for being there. The bishop listened and praised Nic for wanting to do something about the property where his uncle had died. He expressed his sorrow over all of it. She couldn't imagine Nic being turned down until he mentioned the idea of reconstructing the chapel part of the burned church. It would be nondenominational so anyone could use it to pray. At that point the bishop shook his head.

"A chapel of any kind would throw more fuel on an old fire."

On hearing that, she pressed Nic's arm

and whispered, "Do you mind if I say something?"

"Go ahead."

She sat forward. "As Monsieur Causcelle explained, I'm one of the Causcelle corporate attorneys. What he doesn't realize is that I would have advised him against having any kind of chapel built inside. After what happened here, I agree it would be unwise.

"But what you don't know is that Monsieur Causcelle plans to purchase more properties to build hotel hospitals with research centers around France. All will be *free* to the patients and their families with no restrictions as to race, nationality or religion. The acquisition of your property would represent the first one."

The bishop's brows lifted in surprise. He gazed at Nic in wonder.

On a burst of inspiration, Anelise continued. "Each facility will be in honor of the men who lost their lives here, but it will be the Causcelles' secret with God." Having spoken, she sat back and felt Nic's hand grip hers almost painfully, yet she welcomed it.

"You're willing to do this in other parts of France too?" The bishop sounded awestruck.

"It's my father's wish and my hope for the future."

She heard the older man clear his throat. "I'll talk this over with the archbishop when he returns. I won't have an answer for a day or two. My secretary will call you at your corporate offices in Paris, Monsieur Causcelle."

"I can't ask for more than that, Your Reverence. Thank you for seeing us on such short notice."

"It's been my pleasure."

With her fingers crossed, Anelise thanked him and got to her feet.

Charged with emotions difficult to contain, Nic walked her out of the church to the car in the parking lot. Before he helped her in, he wanted to crush her in his arms, but had to hold back as other people were walking around. "Do you have any idea what just happened in there?"

She glanced at him with anxiety in those ultramarine blue eyes. "I'm afraid I overstepped another boundary." In the next breath she climbed in the front seat while he walked around.

"That's not true," he cried after getting in

behind the wheel. "Your last words to him about my family's secret with God were the exact thoughts in my heart. I couldn't believe it when I heard you voice them. Instead of him turning us away like he's done to my father numerous times, he said he'd talk with the archbishop. You, Anelise Lavigny, accomplished something I didn't think was possible. It's a first step and I'm indebted to you."

"I refuse to take credit for anything. I saw his eyes, Nic. When I told him you were going to build these facilities in other parts of France—when he realized they would be free to anyone needing help—your words spoke to *his* heart."

Anelise quickly looked away from him. "I can testify that you *are* your father's son. Now I think we'd better go or we'll be late. Your sister said we'd be eating dinner early."

The last thing Nic wanted was to share her with anyone else, but Corinne had gathered the family around their father. "Let's not say anything about this in case nothing comes of it."

She nodded.

"Anelise? Tomorrow morning, I have something I have to do and will be away for a couple of hours. Just so you know, I'll be back in time for lunch."

"That's fine. If your father is up to it, we'll have a visit."

"He'll love that."

When they returned to the château, she disappeared upstairs and didn't come down until Nic knocked on her door. His other sisters and their families had assembled and greeted Anelise with warmth when they walked in the dining room. Nic had her sit down next to him.

Their father took over. "Nicolas has informed me that he and Anelise are not engaged, only pretending to be until they can speak to the person who had lies about them printed in the newspaper. What's nice is that Anelise works for our corporation, so she won't be leaving us."

"I've never seen such a big diamond!" This from sixteen-year-old Brigitte, one of Corinne's children.

Anelise removed the ring and passed it around so everyone could examine it. "It's huge!" Julie cried. She was Yvette's sixteen-year-old daughter.

"Your *oncle* has exquisite taste."

"Are you going to let her keep it, Oncle Nicolas?"

Good question, one that had kept him awake last night. "If she wants it, it's hers, Brigitte."

"I liked that black Bugatti I saw you driving on the news, Oncle Nicolas. When are you going to let me drive it?" Honore questioned. Corinne's fifteen-year-old son brought smiles to everyone at the table.

"Yeah," called out Theo, a son of Yvette's.

Nic grinned. "When you're old enough to handle such power."

"Was it fun riding in it, Mademoiselle Lavigny?" asked Anne's thirteen-year-old daughter, Lisanne. "I'd give anything!"

Before she could answer, Nic said, "She took one look at it and cried, '*Holy Bugatti!*'"

The whole room exploded in laughter, including Anelise. He couldn't remember when they'd ever been this happy as a family.

"It's true," Anelise claimed with tears of laughter in her eyes. "I was convinced your *oncle* was a new version of Batman." Her charm infected everyone, including him.

"I guess I'll have to drive it here one day and take you all for a ride."

"Yay!" the kids shrieked with excitement.

His gaze sought Anelise's eyes. Hers shimmered like sea glass. He knew she was enjoying this too.

After dessert he whispered, "Would you like to take a short drive before bed?" He was aching to hold and kiss her.

"That sounds lovely, but I'm tired and plan to do some reading. How about tomorrow?" She got up from the table.

Nic rose to his feet. He fought to keep the disappointment out of his voice. "We'll do whatever you'd like."

"I'd love to see the *fromagerie* where the little photo of you and your brothers was taken."

He couldn't understand her fascination with that photo, but his question about it would have to wait. "I'll put it on our agenda."

"You have a wonderful family and I bet your father is anxious to spend some private time with you. *Bonne nuit*, Nic."

She thanked Corinne for the delicious lamb dinner and said good-night to everyone before leaving the room.

Nic watched her go. For reasons he didn't understand, Anelise wanted to be alone. Tomorrow he would get to the bottom of it. He turned to push his father's wheelchair to his suite on the main floor of the château. After a short visit because Louis was tired, Nic went to his suite on the second floor and phoned Raoul.

His brother picked up after the first ring. "Nic—I'm glad you called. I've been anxious to know how everything went with Papa."

"I buried the hatchet, and he wept with me. He agrees on my pretending to be engaged to Anelise until we confront the culprit. I told him we've got Claude on the job looking for Jean-Louis. That's how it went."

"I couldn't be happier," his brother said in a husky voice. Nic had to hold back about the visit to the bishop until he had answers.

"Any news from Claude?"

"Not yet."

"I'll be back tomorrow night and we'll talk then. *A demain.*"

They clicked off and he went up to his room. When he finally climbed in bed, his mind kept returning to that moment at the table with Anelise. Until he'd asked her to go for a drive with him, he'd felt she wanted to be with him in all ways. Why did she unexpectedly pull away?

Nic tossed and turned, going over everything in his mind. There'd been so many moments where he'd felt a closeness with her. He'd never experienced those kinds of feelings with another woman. How could he forget her words to the bishop? She'd been so in sync with Nic's emotions, it was uncanny. He couldn't have imagined her sudden breathlessness when they touched, or the way she'd look through to his soul with those incredible blue eyes.

He pounded his pillow, trying to find a position so he would fall asleep, but it was a long time in coming. Relieved when morning arrived, he showered and shaved. Once dressed in a suit and tie, he left the château for the dairy. Since there'd been a breakthrough with the bishop, Nic hoped the same might be true with old man Dumotte, the head of the dairy, for Raoul's sake. Anelise had given Nic hope.

CHAPTER SEVEN

Sunlight streamed through the château windows. Anelise got up to shower and change into jeans and a khaki blouse, always remembering to wear the ring. She tied her hair back at the nape with a scarf and went downstairs.

The Leclerc children had already gone to school. Though she enjoyed talking to Louis and Corinne after breakfast, Anelise kept waiting for Nic, who ought to be back from his errand by now. The fact that she cared so much alarmed her. She'd hoped morning would help her to think clearly about the situation with a man who wasn't her fiancé. To her chagrin, she realized Nic had become important to her in a way that frightened her.

As she'd told her parents, he was a troubled man with issues. He'd never loved his former fiancée. Maybe he couldn't love any woman. Perhaps the absence of a mother interacting with his father had affected his vision of marital love.

Neither Nic nor his brothers had married yet. That was why it would be ridiculous for her to get involved emotionally with a man who wasn't interested in her. Forget that he was one of France's most famous celebrities. In the end it could only mean heartache for her. She'd had enough of that with the loss of Andre.

The sooner they learned more about Babette Lafrenière's background and dealt with her, the better. Then this charade would be over. Anelise had promised to continue working for the Causcelle Corporation, but she'd find a new place to live on her own.

"There you are, *mon fils*!"

Nic had just walked in the salon to hug his father. Anelise's pulse came to life.

Corinne stood up. "Can I get you something to eat, Nic?"

"*Non, merci.* I ate earlier, and I've promised to show Anelise the countryside. We need to get going since we have to return to Paris tonight."

"Then you two go on and enjoy yourselves," Louis said, smiling at her.

"I've loved talking to both of you." Anelise got up to follow Nic out of the château to his car.

He helped her get in. "We'll drive north, then head back to the *fromagerie*. Sorry I was so long."

"Don't be. Did you accomplish what you needed to do this morning?"

"No."

"I'm sorry," she said when he gave no explanation. Something was troubling him. "While you were gone, your father and sister gave me a history of your family that kept me fascinated. You mentioned he has a brother Blaise who's a professor of Latin and Greek at the Sorbonne. How different could the interests of two brothers be?"

"The university life always appealed to him. His son, Pascal, a married cousin my age, runs a printing company in Paris and publishes many of his father's works while he helps me and Raoul. They and their families can't get enough of the big city."

"Paris *is* wonderful."

"Speaking of Paris, do you know you haven't told me about your life growing up. Where were you born?"

"In Paris. When I got older, I spent holidays with my mother's wonderful parents in Orleans."

"What about Hugo's parents?"

"They lived in Paris. Papa's mother died when I was seven. My grandfather passed away from the *grippe* during my first year in high school. I loved them so much."

His eyes found hers. "What about aunts, uncles and cousins?"

"Our families weren't prolific like yours, Nic. Papa was their only child, and my mother only had one sister who died soon after being born. But I'm not complaining. No girl ever had a more wonderful childhood than I did. My mother let me bring all my girlfriends home from school and have sleepovers. We used to play school. I ended up being the teacher and thought I'd grow up to be one."

"What happened that you didn't?"

"You really want to know?"

"I want to learn everything about the brilliant woman my father hired. He's always had a sixth sense and knew he'd found gold when he found you."

She didn't dare take those words to heart, but they thrilled her nonetheless. "I was in my last year of high school and my father had a problem that not even his best attorney could solve. He had to ask around for someone exceptional and it cost him a fortune. One night I peeked in his study and caught him pacing. He looked at me and said, "You know what I need, Annie girl? If you go into law, you could be my attorney and help me when I get into trouble. No one sees a problem the way you do. You're a marvel.'

"I knew he was teasing, but I also knew he rarely brought his troubles home. It hit me then how much he carried on his shoulders no one knew about. I started thinking about what he'd said, and weeks later I made the decision to go to law school after graduation. I wanted to be able to help him one day the way he'd always helped me."

After a silence, "Did his attorney prevail?" Nic asked in an oddly thick toned voice.

"Yes."

He reached for her hand. "Thank you for letting me look into that Lavigny *tranche de vie*. The more I find out about you, the more I realize how remarkable you really are."

"If you're not careful, you're going to make me cry."

"Then we'll change the subject." He let go of her, but she wished he hadn't. "Take a look at the land around here. It's home to me and my siblings. Always will be. Do you know this is the only place in France that produces all the wine types? *Vin de paille, rose, jaune, rouge and blanc.* The quality of the soil makes the difference."

"After what you told me earlier today, you really should have been able to go into research."

"I'm not complaining. Not anymore."

The new understanding with his father had done wonders for his morale and she was happy for him. "Where are we going exactly?"

"I thought I'd show you a place most people never visit whether they're a native or a tourist."

"But *you* have, Nic."

"Our father made certain of it to further our education. It's a site called Seine-Source, the beginning of the Seine river. Since you've never been there, I thought you'd like to see where it starts out in a wooded area as a tiny trickle."

"The world-famous Seine a *trickle*?"

Her comment produced a chuckle. Before long they reached the spring and the artificial grotto above that comprised a dragon, a dog and a statue of a nymph called Sequana. "My *oncle* would tell you it's Latin for snake."

"The river does meander like one!" she murmured. "Jacqueline Francois immortalized it in the song called 'La Seine.' I've always adored the words."

"Do you remember them?"

"Only the ending. I think it goes, 'She sings her love for Paris because the Seine is a lover and Paris sleeps in her bed.'"

Nic pinned her with his intense gaze. "The author of those words had to be in love. You told me that your love for Andre was real. How did you meet him? Or would you rather not talk about him?"

"I don't mind." It didn't hurt, not anymore. "I had a law study group and one of the girls gave a party. She invited some other friends. Andre happened to be among them, an engineering student. He played a lot of tennis and asked me if I'd like to spend one afternoon away from the books and have a game with him."

"Which obviously you did."

She laughed. "We had many of them."

"He must have fallen in love with you on the spot."

By the way he was looking at her, and the

throb in his vibrant voice, Anelise couldn't swallow, let alone talk. She wasn't thinking about Andre. Her mind kept visualizing the Seine swirling around Paris where she and Nic lay locked in each other's arms. This had to stop. "I guess we'd better get going."

"One more spot to see."

He drove south while he talked about the history of the area back in the 1200s. He knew everything! When they reached the large cheese-making plant, Nic parked near it. "We're facing the pasture where that photo was taken, but there are no cows right now. I'd take you on a tour of the place, but we have to pack and drive fifteen miles to the airport."

"I know." It was for the best, but she wanted to cry her eyes out for having to leave. Being with Nic had given her a new sense of confidence, and made her see some strengths that she'd never considered. He'd opened her eyes to a different sort of life.

"Tell me something, Anelise. Why were you so interested in the photo of this place my father showed you?"

"Not only the place, Nic. Most women think about being married and having children. When I saw those three adorable faces and realized your father had to take over from day one, it touched my heart. Both of your parents had to make sacrifices. She took care of your three sisters while she carried her sons in the womb. Your father did the rest. It's a success story beyond comprehension. That was the day I recognized the true meaning of the word *sacrifice*."

All went quiet until he let out a deep sigh. "You've made me look at everything in a new light. I'm more grateful than you know."

He'd just spoken the words in her heart. After that admission, he started the car and they headed for the château to get their bags and say goodbye.

She studied his profile, recognizing she wasn't the same woman who'd flown here yesterday. Stepping into Nic's world had changed her until she didn't know herself.

All Nic could think of during the flight to Paris was that Anelise would be going back to his suite with him. They would have total privacy. When it came time to work at the office, she'd be with him. Until they investigated Babette and decided what to do about her, he would keep Anelise to himself day and night for as long as he wanted. He didn't

have to be in a hurry. She wasn't going anywhere.

The minute his driver had taken them to
the *palais* and they'd reached his suite, she
turned to him. "Nic? I hope you're going
to contact that PI about Mademoiselle
Lafrenière right away."

"First thing in the morning."

"Good. I have visions of her showing up
in my office to confront me. That woman
doesn't worry about boundaries."

Her comment gave him the impetus to tell
her of his idea that had been percolating for
several days. "While we're pretending to be
engaged, I'm moving you into my office with
me. If she comes barging in, she'll have to
face me."

"No, Nic. You're the CEO. It wouldn't be
right. Surely we don't have to go *that* far."

He eyed her. "You didn't hear all the things
she said to me at the car dealership. Want to
bet she won't show up tomorrow?"

She looked down. "No. I trust your in-
stincts."

"Bon," he muttered with satisfaction. "It's
settled. Now that we're back, please help
yourself to anything in the kitchen while I

phone my brother." Claude would be getting a call from him too.

"Thank you, Nic, but the food on the plane did it for me. I had a wonderful time. See you in the morning." She disappeared into her bedroom.

He stared after her until she shut the door. Frustrated with longings he'd never experienced for any woman, he charged into his room and changed into a robe.

His hand gripped his cell harder. "Come on, Raoul. Answer!" The phone rang five times before his brother picked up sounding drowsy.

"*Eh bien.* Are you still in La Racineuse?"

"We just got back. Have you talked to Claude?"

"No. He left me a message that he's out of town, but will call as soon as he has any information. Are you all right? You sound anxious. Is Papa worse?"

Nic took a quick breath. "For now, he seems fine. We had the most amazing visit of our lives and I've made my peace with him."

"Is that the truth?"

"I don't blame you for being skeptical."

"How did he handle that hideous article and your fake engagement?"

"He said he was glad it happened since it brought him and me together. But what I'd like to know is how *you're* handling the endless buzz, Raoul."

"It's all anyone talks about."

"I'm sorry."

After a brief silence, "Did you—"

"No luck," Nic cut him off.

A telling sigh came through the phone.

"Sorry, bro." Nic cleared his throat and changed the subject. "Do me a favor? As soon as Claude gets back to you, tell him to phone me. I have another job for him that's critical too."

"What's going on?"

"Guess who's our culprit."

"I can't imagine."

"Babette Lafrenière."

"I don't know that name."

Nic let out a laugh. "You don't watch much TV either. That's what Anelise said when she met her for the first time."

"Raoul—let me in on your joke."

"Babette is a *vedette* in some TV series. The information on the web says she's French-Canadian, but she gives no evidence of it in her speech. Anelise and I believe she could be dangerous. That's why I need to get in touch with Claude. I want her investigated before I decide what to do."

"I'll send him another message and ask him to get started on her ASAP."

"You're the best. *Bonne nuit.*"

Anelise brought the rest of her things from her office into Nic's. He'd had her desk and equipment moved early that morning. Now they sat opposite each other. He smiled like a cat who'd just eaten a bowl full of tuna. "I'm crazy about this arrangement. We can see each other every second."

As if she weren't aware of it and loving it. His outrageous comments made her laugh. They also caused her heart to ping throughout the morning. He ordered lunch and snacks for them. She'd never had so much fun in her life, on or off the job.

Nic had to answer more calls than she could imagine. Her admiration for his knowledge and business acumen continued to grow at an alarming rate.

At four, George buzzed Nic. "You have a visitor again," he said in a hushed tone. "She insists on seeing *you*." Eyes black as India ink sought Anelise with that I-told-you-so look. "Shall I call for security?"

"That won't be necessary, George. Walk her down the hall to my office."

"Tres bien."

Clicking off, Nic sat back in his leather chair. "Let's play her along and see what happens."

Anelise's hand tightened on the pen she'd been using to make notes on a possible new hotel acquisition. The numbers didn't add up. She needed more information on the demographics and needed to talk to Nic about it. "As long as I have your back."

"Is there any question of it?"

"Of course not, Nic. But I *am* concerned she's baiting you. She has no fear of reprisal."

"Which proves she's a threat. We'll figure it out. All you have to do is take your cues from me."

A knock on the door ended the discussion. *"Entrez."*

When the door opened, Babette came in without invitation, but stopped when she saw Anelise and the diamond on her ring finger. "I asked to see *you*, Nic Causcelle, not the new attorney."

"I'm sure you know that Anelise is my fiancée and I can't bear to be apart from her." It had been all over the news. Knowing of her obsession, he couldn't tell if she was feigning ignorance or not, but it didn't matter. "How can I help you? Advice on another car perhaps?"

Her head reared. "I want to live in the *palais*. It's near the film studio where I can get away from my fans. There are times when I need peace. The security guards make it the perfect place for privacy."

Anelise stepped in. "I'm afraid you won't get much peace if you live there, Mademoiselle Lafrenière. Nic can't make a move without someone out in the parking area shoving a camera or a microphone in his face. When I think about it, you must have tremendous confidence to perform for an audience the way you do and deal with all the adulation. I know *I* couldn't do it."

Nic smiled at Anelise. "As long as you remember *I'm* your doting audience, *ma belle*, nothing else matters." He sounded like he really meant it, and his eyes played over her with such a slow intimacy, it robbed her of breath. They might as well have been the only two in the room before he eventually stood up and transferred his attention to Babette.

"The *palais* isn't a hotel, Mademoiselle

Lafrenière. It's the home where the Caus-celle family has resided for over a hundred years. Only members of my family stay there when they are in Paris."

She glared at Anelise. "*She* lives there."

"Because my father made it possible. She's a special case and was installed in one of my sister's suites when he hired her to work for the corporation. Soon she'll be his daughter-in-law and he adores her." Nic sought Anelise's gaze once more. "So do I, and now she's living with me."

"And I love it," Anelise said in a trembly voice. It was only the truth.

The other woman glared at her with eyes spouting nonverbal vitriol. The actress hadn't yet figured out what was going on, not when she'd thought she'd destroyed Nic with her lies.

"My fiancée and I wish you luck in your career, Mademoiselle Lafrenière. Now if you'll excuse us, we're busy trying to get some work done." He walked toward the door and opened it.

Dead silence on the *vedette*'s part meant nothing had gone the way she'd imagined when she'd barged in. Anelise got the feeling Babette wanted to stomp her foot and start throwing things like the little girl with the curl. She did neither. With an imperious turn of her head, she marched out.

Nic closed the door behind her and took a few long strides to his desk to make a phone call. "Robert? Mademoiselle Lafrenière might be coming by. I've told her it won't be possible for her to move in. If she gives you any trouble, let me know." He hung up.

"What an amazing woman!" Anelise cried, trying hard not to laugh out loud. "Poor Robert if he has to tangle with her again."

Nic's features darkened. "She's bold beyond caring, Anelise. More than ever, we know she's up to something that could be criminal. She wants a lot more than a room at the *palais*."

"I know. I keep wondering what she hopes to achieve now that we've called her bluff. We haven't fooled her. No doubt she has more tricks up her sleeve and will now be ready to play them. I'm starting to get nervous."

"We've got security and you've got me. I'm Batman, remember?"

"This isn't funny, Nic. If anything happened to you—"

Something flickered in the recesses of his

eyes as he stared at her. "Nothing will happen to either of us. Raoul has contacted the man who is looking into her background for us. It won't be long before we discover the truth. But I don't want to think about her right now. What do you say we quit for the day and drive out of the city for dinner?"

Yes, yes. "I'd love it, but before we leave, I'm trying to solve a problem with a case Serge assigned me. The figures don't match the asking price of this older hotel your father wants to buy. I'd like your opinion."

"Where is it located?"

"At the Quartier Saint Louis District in Versailles."

"Versailles? That's perfect. I'll have my car brought around and we'll discuss it en route. Once we've checked everything out, we'll do what Marie Antoinette did."

"You mean visit the farm and dairy when she could?"

He nodded. "Where else? It's my favorite place on the estate. We'll see the cows we didn't have time to see out at La Racineuse. Maybe some sheep too. The last time I was there they dressed up the sheep in ribbons."

"You're kidding."

He laughed. "Raoul considered that an

insult because the farm wasn't a pretense for the queen. She'd loved it and wanted her royal children to love it too. I haven't been there in ages."

Neither had Anelise. Doing anything with Nic gave her an ecstatic feeling she wouldn't be able to hide from him much longer.

CHAPTER EIGHT

Nic drove into the town of Versailles and they reached the old Peacock Inn Hotel. Once a favorite spot in the reign of Louis XIV, it now appeared on its last legs.

"What's the financial history on the place, Anelise?"

"According to this report, the latest owner died without children. No one came forward to keep it in condition and it became a liability to the bank. They've had it up for sale for twenty years."

"Does it say why my father decided to buy it?"

"Yes. He received a favorable report from the chief engineer on the property. The foundation is solid and the ground stable. Therefore, remodeling could go ahead without problem. Serge added the following note about your father's reasons. 'It's near Louis

XIII's former deer park, the Saint Louis cathedral and the King's Kitchen Garden.'"

"Papa loves his history."

"But I don't think he'll love the asking price. I've done research on the other real estate properties sold in this neighborhood in the last year. Their tax bases aren't high, yet none of the transactions reveal the sold prices. That goes against the public freedom of information act. I've a feeling the bank is asking for an exorbitant amount of money here."

"Naturally. With Papa as the buyer, they can make up for the taxes and money for improvements they've had to invest to hold on to it for the last twenty years. No doubt they've leaned on the owners of the sold properties to keep quiet."

"That's illegal, Nic."

"I suspect they're relying on an ancient law about this being part of a royal holding to support their position. If that's the case, we'll fight it. First you'll need to contact Jacques Beauvais in the Yvelines Ile-de-France Department."

"I'll spend tomorrow sending out information requests to him and we'll see what happens."

"Tell him we'll go to court if we have to before I sign anything. And now, I'm tired of thinking and want to enjoy the rest of the day with you." And the evening, *and* the night. All he could think about was being alone with her.

When they reached the mammoth château, visiting hours had ended. Tourists were leaving in droves. Nic held her arm while they walked through the unique grounds. Though beautiful, he preferred to watch her expression as she took it all in.

"Do you know the scroll designs of this garden around the water *parterre* remind me of stained-glass window outlines? Maybe Le Nôtre had them in mind when he created this masterpiece."

"Maybe," he murmured, but right now he was too fascinated by the way the sun brought out the different colors in her silky dark blond hair. Strange how he'd thought she'd had light brown hair when he'd first seen her walking to work.

They continued on toward the Queen's Hamlet and stood beneath the trees. "Oh, Nic… We're too late to visit the dairy."

He slid his arm around her womanly waist, wanting to feel her close to his body. "I'm disappointed too. We'll come back next week and make a day of it."

"Could we?" She turned her head and that's when their cheeks brushed, stoking the fire burning inside him. He pulled her into his arms. "Forgive me, Anelise, but I can't hold off any longer." In the next breath he lowered his head and covered those enticing lips that had been calling to him like a siren.

All day he'd imagined kissing her while they sat across from each other in his office. Now he had his heart's desire and didn't want it to end. He knew instinctively she'd wanted this too. Their transforming kiss grew deeper and longer. He wanted to carry her someplace and love her into oblivion until a voice called out that they needed to leave.

Nic had a hard time relinquishing her delectable mouth and body. A blush crept into her cheeks the second the guard on duty walked up to them. The man's eyes widened.

"It's *you*, Monsieur Causcelle!" His eyes swept over Anelise with male appreciation. "Forgive me for intruding on you and your fiancée, but the gates closed at six and now it's seven thirty. I'll phone security to let you out."

"That's very kind of you. *Merci.*" He grasped

her hand and they retraced their steps across the grounds to the entrance.

"Even an estate guard knows who you are, Monsieur Causcelle," she teased.

Once past the gate he said, "I'm sorry, Anelise. You had me so enthralled, I didn't notice the time, let alone anyone else around."

"Neither of us did." She took a breath, seemingly to steady herself. "Even if you felt you had to work for your father in the business, I don't know why you didn't disappear years ago like your brother."

"I'm glad I didn't, otherwise I would never have met you." Her eyes widened at his words. After helping her into his black Mercedes, they left the parking area. "You have a knack for changing the subject when you're uncomfortable, Mademoiselle Lavigny. But I'm not going to apologize for what went on between us back there."

She didn't look at him. "I'm afraid it was inevitable. We've been virtually living together for a week. The night we got engaged I had a difficult time remembering that the way you kissed and held me wasn't real." After a pause, "You can understand why some film stars carry on off-screen for a while after playing the kind of romantic role we've undertaken."

For a while? Her admission meant he hadn't been dreaming about the feelings they'd aroused in each other from the moment they'd met.

"Let's drive back by the Peacock. I saw a place where we could have dinner."

She turned to him. "Now who's changing the subject? You're spooking *me* if you're talking about the Creperie. I've been salivating ever since I saw it."

"There was no other place to eat." Their minds *did* think alike.

A few minutes later he pulled up in front of the small restaurant and they went inside. To his relief no one recognized him. He asked the young waitress for a table in the rear for privacy. She handed them menus.

Nic glanced at his and knew what he wanted. "Have you seen something that appeals to you, Anelise?"

"The Louis galettes sound delicious. They're stuffed with ground beef and eggs. I'd also like cappuccino, even if it isn't French."

The waitress came back. "Are you ready to order?"

"*Oui.* How large are the galettes?"

"One is enough for me."

"*Bon.* One for my fiancée, and two for me. Both of us want cappuccino."

"*A toute à l'heure*, monsieur." She walked away.

A smile lifted one corner of Anelise's mouth. "You've gained another admirer in your miles-long list. She couldn't take her eyes off you."

As long as Anelise liked looking at him, nothing else mattered. "I told her you were my fiancée."

"She didn't care I was wearing this ring. You're a regular hazard, Nic."

A laugh escaped. "Is that what you think about me?"

"Yes. You should walk around in a ski mask."

"That's fine. I'll only take it off for you."

"Nic…" Her voice had gone husky.

He loved the sometimes shy side of her.

Their food arrived. After eating one galette, he stared at her over the rim of his coffee. "I have an idea. Tomorrow's Saturday. I need to be in work for the day to catch up, but let's do something exciting afterward."

She'd just taken another bite of food and

had to swallow. "I can't. It's my aunt's birthday. I'll spend the day at work too, but I'm driving to Orleans with my folks tomorrow evening and will be staying through Sunday."

The news that she'd be away from Paris for the rest of the weekend came as a blow. "Does your aunt know about us?"

"Everyone believes we're engaged, and I'll go on wearing the ring. Just be thankful you don't have to be dragged along to keep up the pretense."

This was no longer a pretense for Nic, but he didn't know what the hell to do about it yet. He finished the second galette, but it tasted like sawdust. "If you're ready, let's go."

By quarter to ten they'd arrived back at the *palais*. No sooner had they reached his suite than his cell rang.

She smiled at him. "I bet that's your brother. See you in the morning." She disappeared before he could stop her. He knew why. She didn't want to talk about that kiss near the royal dairy, but he couldn't stop thinking about it. From the first moment he'd seen her walking along the street, he'd felt an attraction that had taken over his whole world.

Since the evening that they'd agreed to get engaged, every look, touch and kiss had brought him to life. She filled his dreams. Within a week, his world had become a different place that exhilarated him. The thought of her not being in it for the rest of his life terrified him.

Anelise checked her watch. One thirty. Sleep wouldn't come. Not tonight. The reason for her agony slept in another bedroom. Much as she would like to blame it on anything but the truth, she couldn't.

Be honest with yourself, Anelise. You're in love with him, a man you've only known a week, but he's not in love with you.

Nic had admitted that his engagement to Denise hadn't been a true love affair. He'd let her go. The only reason he'd asked Anelise to play along with the fake engagement had to do with Babette Lafrenière. His hormones had nothing to do with love. In twenty-nine years neither Nic nor his brothers had married.

He and Raoul seemed to get along better than most married couples, and their greatest concerns involved their father and Jean-Louis. She needed to face it. Three devastatingly attractive, brilliant men, wealthy beyond comprehension, continued to remain single for a reason she didn't understand.

Anelise pummeled her pillow. No more living here in Nic's suite while she ached to be in his arms and kissed forever. After the party tonight in Orleans, she would come back to Paris on Sunday and get an apartment near the Sacre Coeur, a favorite area. She wouldn't see Nic until she went to work Monday morning.

With her mind made up, she turned on her other side and prayed for oblivion. To her shock she awakened the next morning realizing she'd finally slept, but she'd be late for work. Thank heaven Nic had already left when she emerged from the bedroom.

After grabbing a cup of coffee, she hurried outside with her briefcase and practically ran to the office. Nic, freshly shaven, sat at his desk, already on the phone with someone. In a light gray suit and tie, he looked so handsome it hurt.

"Sorry I'm late, Nic."

He'd just gotten off the phone and flashed her a smile to die for. "You work too hard and should have slept all day."

"I couldn't. These request forms need to be finished and couriered by afternoon."

"I'll help you since Claude will be coming here at two to give us the lowdown on Babette."

"Oh—" she cried in surprise. "Did he say anything about her?"

One dashing black brow lifted. "Only that our suspicions are dead-on."

The news gave her hope the situation would be resolved in the next day or two. They could get on with their separate lives. She'd leave the *palais*, and move back to her own office. That way she'd only see Nic once in a while.

She got to work and before she knew it, the requests they'd worked on had gone out. Nic ordered lunch and then Claude arrived. With the introductions made, he put on his glasses and pulled some papers out of his valise.

"This is a fascinating case. First of all, she's been having a liaison with a journalist at *Paris Now*. The business printed on the internet is fiction. She wasn't born in French Canada. Her birth mother, now deceased eight years, was Eva Grenier, of Lyons, France. She had a baby out of wedlock.

"The daughter, Babette Grenier Hoang, is

twenty-nine, not twenty-four. The birth father was the notorious Henri Duong Hoang from Vietnam. He was imprisoned in Turkey for robbery. Later released. Fled to Lyons, France, where he met Eva and got involved in a big gambling operation in Paris. He killed a man that didn't pay his gambling debt." Claude eyed the two of them. "That killing took place at the café-bar where both your fathers were eating."

"Nic—" she cried in astonishment. Their gazes met in disbelief.

"There's more," Claude continued. "The police caught up with Henri, who went to prison and died there three months ago from strangulation. According to prison records, Babette visited him there regularly.

"Several inmates testified that his daughter never forgave Louis Causcelle for helping the police put her father in prison. He identified the ring with a snake insignia. His daughter has the same design tattooed on her right calf. She knew her birth father was the killer, but she doesn't care.

"She has performed on TV, but in a minor role and the show was canceled. To my knowledge she doesn't have another job yet. She's living in rooms at the back of the Fusion Bar in Pigalle. Apparently she has an uncle in Lyons who works in a bar. Maybe there's a connection."

Nic rose to his feet. "She hates my father and has been planning her revenge. It makes horrific sense. Claude? I can't thank you enough for all you've done so quickly. You know you can name your price."

He got to his feet. "I'll leave this information with you. There's enough here for you to prosecute her for the lie in the paper. I only wish I had better news on your brother. I'm still working with one military man who I believe can tell us what we want to know about Jean-Louis. The minute I hear from him, I'll let you know."

After he left, Nic walked around and pulled Anelise into his arms. She couldn't deny him right now and they clung. "You were right about her. Our culprit has been living in a world of hurt neither of us can imagine."

"I can't comprehend what she's been through in her life."

"If I know you, you don't want her prosecuted. Neither do I. Let's go back to the *palais* and decide what we're going to do. But first I need this."

He trapped her mouth with his and kissed her so hungrily, she could hardly breathe. This wasn't supposed to happen, not if he didn't love her. Afraid of her own feelings, she slowly eased away from him. A good walk back to the *palais* would help her work off the emotions riddling her.

Part of her felt great relief that they knew what had driven Babette's agenda and why. Yet the other part of her suffered pain because this meant there was no more need for the engagement. His desire for her didn't mean love. No doubt he'd kissed Denise with this much passion, enjoying the moment. But it wasn't enough for Anelise.

The whole purpose of the engagement had been to expose the culprit. Now that Babette had been flushed out, Nic no longer required Anelise's cooperation. The birthday party for her aunt couldn't have come at a more propitious moment. If she didn't get away from Nic this weekend, she'd never want to leave him.

Could there be anything more pathetic than to hang on to a man when you knew it was hopeless? Denise had been wise enough to figure out the truth in time to find love with another man who would love her back.

Anelise knew deep down she'd never meet a man like Nic in this life, but she didn't want to live in constant pain because he couldn't return her love.

Carrying that thought to its conclusion, it meant she couldn't go on working for the corporation, even though it would hurt her father. Over the weekend she would explain the situation to her parents and hope they would understand.

"Where are you going?" Nic asked after they'd walked in the suite.

"To pack an overnight bag."

He frowned. "You can't leave yet. We need to talk about Babette."

She didn't want to go anywhere, but she had to get out of here for self-preservation. "I know. Give me five minutes first."

Five turned into fifteen before she entered the salon with a suitcase and sat down on a chair. Nic had made himself comfortable on the couch in shirtsleeves. He'd been writing what appeared to be a letter.

"You've been busy."

Nic looked up at her. "I thought I'd have this sent to her and would like your opinion." He handed it to her.

Great penmanship was a lost art these days, but not for Nic.

Chère Mademoiselle Babette Grenier Hoang,
My fiancée and I want to express our sorrow over the loss of your mother, Eva, and your father, Henri. Your life must seem even more difficult to be told your series was canceled. We have every hope you'll be asked to do another one soon. God bless you in the future.
Sincerely, Nicolas and Anelise

Tears threatened, blurring her eyes. She put the letter on the coffee table and stood up. "Babette will be shocked out of her mind that you know everything about her and figured out she was the one who had the lie printed. The fact that you're not seeking retribution of any kind should silence anyone with even a modicum of decency.

"The journalist at *Paris Now* she's been seeing will tell her she's lucky to have received a gracious letter like that rather than a summons to appear in court. It's perfect, Nic." *You're* perfect.

"Your approval means a great deal since you were attacked too."

"Thank goodness it's over. Now I have to leave. My parents are waiting for me. See you Monday at work."

"You won't be coming back here Sunday night?"

She shook her head. "No. I have other plans. Now that we know about Babette, you should be able to enjoy your weekend. *A la prochaine.*"

Anelise left the suite so fast, Nic didn't have time to take a breath. But right now wasn't the time to stop her. He'd received several calls. One from the bishop, another from Raoul and one from his sister Yvette he needed to return. Maybe their father had grown worse. The letter he intended to courier to Babette could wait until tomorrow.

He reached for the phone and called her. "Yvette? Is it bad news about Papa?"

"I'm glad you called. No. This is about Oncle Raimond. It's very sad. He fell at the *ferme* today. Stefan got him to the hospital. The doctors say he has a bad case of ALS."

Nic groaned. Raimond was their father's younger brother by a year.

"As you know, he's been in charge of everything at La Racineuse for years. This news means the workers under him will have to manage. Unfortunately, there isn't anyone to do the job the way he has done it, and his son Stefan is needed at the *fromagerie*. Papa says you're in charge, Nic. Do you have any suggestions?"

Yes, and he was going to do something about it right now. "I've got several calls to make, then I'll phone you back with an answer."

"Bless you, *mon frere*."

After they clicked off, he scanned his phone list for his dynamo cousin Pascal and rang him. Ten minutes later he called him back. "*Eh bien, Nic—comment ca va?* Congratulations on your engagement. She's one gorgeous woman."

"You think?" They both laughed. Everyone in the family liked Pascal, including Nic. "I'm calling as the head of the Causcelle Corporation. Do you understand what I'm saying?"

After a silence, "I think I do."

"I was wondering if you would take over for Raoul at headquarters. I don't know for how long and I can't give you more than a minute to think about it."

"You're kidding me."

"I wish I were, but the situation is serious. I can't think of another person, let alone a family member, who could do Raoul's job and then some the way you could. But only if you want to."

He heard a slight intake of breath. "I'm your man."

"That's what I needed to hear. I'll call you back by the end of the evening to make it official."

Three seconds later he phoned Raoul. "I'm on my way over to your suite. Don't go anywhere!"

He left his suite through a side door and ran down the hall where Raoul stood waiting for him. "What's going on?"

Nic grabbed his brother. "I've got something to tell you, so just listen and don't say a word until I'm finished."

Five minutes later Raoul gave him a bear hug he'd always remember.

Nic knew what this moment meant to him. "While you phone Pascal and catch him up on what's important before you leave for La Racineuse, I'll phone Yvette with the news."

"Nic? I have no words." His emotions had overcome him.

After another hug Nic walked back to his suite and returned the bishop's call. He learned enough that he couldn't wait to talk the news over with Anelise. But she hadn't been able to get away from Nic fast enough because she was running from him.

He knew how her mind worked. Now that they'd dealt with Babette, she planned to give him back the ring and move out of his suite. She wanted to end the engagement, but he refused to let that happen.

The hours of the night went on forever without her there. He kept busy until it was time to drive to Orleans on Sunday. It was located on the Loire River, and he thought of the town as Jeanne d'Arc territory. Following the map, he arrived at the beautiful home of Anelise's family on her mother's side. The ivory-toned *chatellerie* sat back in a wooded, sylvan park near a large pond.

Her older blue Peugeot stood out among the luxury cars assembled in the courtyard. Love of money and titles didn't drive her. He'd only been with her for a week, but knew in his gut she was his soul mate. Deep down, he was sure she knew it too. They suited each other and the woman never disappointed.

He got out of the car and walked up to the entrance. A middle-aged housekeeper opened the door. "*Oui*, monsieur?"

"I'm Nicolas Causcelle, the fiancé of Anelise. Will you let her know I'm here?"

"*Tres bien. Entrez.*"

He stepped inside the foyer and looked around. The interior of the beautiful country manor reminded him of his home in La Racineuse. Suddenly he heard footsteps.

"Nic—" She sounded incredulous that he was here.

Anelise walked over to him dressed in a pale blue chambray jumpsuit and heeled sandals. Her dark blond hair floated around her shoulders. Talk about a vision!

"Why didn't you tell me you were coming?" He realized he'd shocked her by showing up like this, yet her eyes shone an azure blue that told him what he needed desperately to know.

"The suite got lonely without you. I decided to surprise you. How's the celebration going?"

"It's over. We've just been in the sun room talking."

"A lot has happened since you left yesterday that I need to talk to *you* about. I'd like to tear you away. Can you leave now? I'll follow you back to Paris."

She hesitated. "I did have other plans."

"You mean about not coming back until Monday? Can't you change them? This is important."

"Does it concern Babette?"

"No. Unless something else happens, she's a thing of the past. I'm talking about news I received from the bishop, as well as an unexpected development in the family. If you're willing, I need your help and it can't wait until Monday."

She took a quick breath. "Of course, I'll do what I can."

"Thank you. Tell you what. I'll go out to my car while you pack. Once back at the *palais* we'll talk everything out." He started for the door.

"Nic—"

He turned to her, afraid she would change her mind if they talked any longer.

"About the bishop. Is it good news?"

"It might be. We'll see."

She dashed off and he left the house. When she didn't appear fifteen minutes later, he realized she was having a difficult time saying goodbye to her family. Nic was about to phone her when she came hurrying out and ran to her car with her suitcase. The sight of her caused him to release the breath he'd been holding. He could have phoned her to talk while they were driving, but decided against it in the heavy traffic.

When they reached the *palais*, he kissed her soft cheek before she climbed out, unable to stop himself. "I know you had other plans for this weekend. This means a lot to me. Thank you, Anelise."

"You don't need to thank me. I want to help you."

CHAPTER NINE

NIC'S APARTMENT HAD never looked so good to him with Anelise planting herself on the couch. He ordered dinner to be set up in the dining room, but would have preferred to grab her and kiss the daylights out of her. However, there were matters to discuss first.

He brought them both a cola from the fridge and sat across from her. "Were your parents disappointed that you had to leave?"

"Not at all. The only thing they were upset about was that I didn't bring you in to meet the rest of the family. I told them you were in a hurry. Now tell me what's wrong."

Nic knew why she didn't want her family seeing him. She was planning to end the engagement, but he had news for her and took a long swallow.

"Raimond Causcelle, *mon oncle*, who lives in La Racineuse, is a year younger than Papa.

For years he has overseen the whole place that includes the *fromagerie*, the livestock, the dairy, the farm, everything! Yesterday he collapsed and the doctors have diagnosed him with a severe case of ALS. He won't ever be able to work again. There's only one person who can take over without a breath being lost. The man I'm talking about will do it in a heartbeat."

"Raoul," she cried out excitedly. "But he runs the other parts of the Causcelle Corporation here in Paris."

"He did until last night when he left for La Racineuse. I've hired our cousin Pascal Causcelle to take his place. I told you about him."

"Yes. You said he's a big entrepreneur."

Anelise had a photographic memory, one of the thousand things he loved about her. "He'll do marvelous innovations with our company. I'll work with him part of the time to help him. We've agreed it's temporary. But it might end up being permanent."

"Incroyable." She recrossed her legs. "Besides the fact that you're losing a brother, how will you be able to do *your* job if you're helping your cousin too?"

"Raoul and I will always be close, but now

I have *you*." He drained the rest of his drink while he let that statement sink in.

A confused expression broke out on her gorgeous face. "What do you mean?"

"For the next week I'm putting you in charge of the hotel division. George will be your backup. He can run everything and has for years. Papa relied on him from the beginning."

She almost dropped her cola. "But what about Serge or Helene?"

"Both are invaluable, but they don't have your brilliance or vision. You take one look at a project and see the merits as well as the flaws. You're like a quarterback in American football. Raoul and I watch our favorite teams every time we can in the autumn. Ever heard of Tom Brady? He looks at the field and knows where he's going to throw the ball before anyone else has even thought about it."

"A quarterback?" She laughed hard. "I've heard of everything now."

He sat forward. "Will you do it? I need you."

"I'm afraid Serge and Helene will be hurt."

Thank heaven they were her only concern. Her kind heart was another trait he adored.

"No, they won't. That's because they trust my judgment and I trust *you*, implicitly. I realize it seems a huge responsibility, but I need you on my team, and I'll be there at the end of the phone if you need me. We'll keep my office just the way it is while we all work together. What's your answer?"

"I'm dumbfounded you'd consider me for this. As long as it's just for a week, I'll go to the office and try to wade through the work you do every day as if it's nothing."

"Is that what I do?"

Her smile melted him to the spot. "Yes. Effortlessly. All men should be so gifted."

"You've made this one very happy."

She put her empty can on the coffee table. "Nic? Don't keep me in suspense. I want to know what the bishop told you."

Nic's heart thundered. "He had a talk with the archbishop and they suggest I present a written, legal contract outlining my plans to their office right away."

Anelise jumped to her feet. "This means they're considering it! You must be thrilled out of your mind."

Almost. "There's just one thing."

"What is it?"

"It's about us." She looked away. "I could

read your mind before you left for Orleans yesterday. We'd dealt with Babette and your eyes said there didn't have to be an 'us' now. We no longer needed to be engaged. That is what you thought. Be honest with me."

She nodded. "It must be a great relief to you."

"You're wrong. I don't want to get unengaged."

Odd how shock suddenly altered her appearance. "Why? I don't understand."

If Anelise only knew how he felt about her, but this wasn't the moment to bare his soul. It had only been a week. She'd never believe he wanted to marry her this fast. "I'm only asking that we stay engaged for a bit longer."

She sank back down on the couch without saying anything.

"What's wrong, Anelise? Is there another man you haven't told me about? Someone you're anxious to be with?"

"You know there isn't!"

"Since you've never talked about your former fiancé, does the memory of your engagement make you feel guilty about ours?" Nic didn't believe it was true, but he had to admit to a certain jealousy over the man who'd won her love.

She looked at him in surprise. "That's not it at all. Nic, if we stay engaged now that Babette's threat is over, it will be dishonest. If you remember, you told me you broke your engagement to Denise because you refused to live a lie when you weren't in love with her. I don't want us to live a lie either."

His body tautened. "That relationship was entirely different than the one you and I are in now. I'm asking you to continue as my fiancée for a specific reason." Long enough for him to convince her he couldn't live without her.

"Raimond's illness is forcing me to navigate through some rough waters. Our family doesn't need the added stress that publicity will create if the press learns our engagement is off. Your role as part of the team will be more credible with you wearing my ring. It adds an essential element of trust."

Again she got up. "I agree you've been thrown a curve you never saw coming and I do agree we should stay engaged for a while longer to avoid more press intrusion. The hierarchy of your corporation is undergoing drastic, major changes that are affecting everyone, including you. I *was* planning to look for a rental tomorrow so I could move out, but you're right. It would create more notoriety you don't need."

"Forgive me if it's asking too much of you. I'm sorry."

"No, no. I'm in this with you all the way. For your sake I'm willing to keep up the pretense until things calm down."

Relief washed through him in waves. "That's all I ask. Dinner has arrived. Let's go in the dining room. While we eat, we can draw up that contract to present to the bishop."

"Do you have specs of the project?"

"I've been working with an architect. They're in my bedroom. I'll get them for you." He came back to the dining room with three scrolls. "Take a look at these."

While they ate and talked, Nic's phone rang. It was Raoul. He picked up. "I didn't expect to hear from you tonight. How are things?"

"So bad you wouldn't believe it. Everything that could go wrong has happened. You need to get out here and help me. The sooner, the better."

Nic took a deep breath. He'd never heard Raoul this shaken. "I'll come first thing in the morning."

"I'll be waiting." He rang off.

Anelise stared at him. "What's wrong, Nic? You look ill. Is your father worse?"

"I don't think so. Raoul only said he needed help. It could mean anything. Let's work on that proposal and get some sleep. I want us to leave here at six in the morning."

Her eyes widened. "You want me to go with you? I thought—"

"I know I wanted you here, but this is an emergency. And while we're in La Racineuse we can visit the bishop. You're the attorney on this project. While you finish working on the contract, I'll phone George and Pascal. They're both going to have to run things tomorrow." He also needed to alert the pilot.

The next morning during the drive from the airport to La Racineuse, Nic told Anelise they would meet his brother at the hospital parking lot. When they arrived, she noticed the place was filled with cars and people. She had no trouble spotting Raoul, who stood out immediately.

This was the first time she'd seen him in person. From a distance they looked identical, but on closer inspection she saw differences. Nic pulled in by his car and they got out.

Raoul walked over to them. "Finally we meet, Anelise." The two brothers were definitely part of a set, but not the same. He kissed her on both cheeks. "Papa raves about you."

"Your brother thinks the world of you."

"It's mutual."

"I've wanted to meet you. I'm sorry about your father and your *oncle*."

"Thank you. We all are. Raimond is worse than we thought and can't have visitors. Maybe tomorrow."

"I was afraid of that," Nic muttered. "More than ever it's important that you're here to take over. Don't worry about anything. Pascal has climbed on board without a murmur. Between you and me, I think he's perfect for the job."

"I couldn't agree more, but now we need to talk."

"That's why I'm here."

"I'll follow you home."

Anelise knew at once Raoul was disappointed she'd come. "I have an idea. Since you have so much to talk about, why don't I follow you?"

Nic flashed her a grateful glance. "You don't mind?"

"What do you think?" She got back in the car and started the engine. The two brothers climbed in Raoul's car and took off. Friends from the cradle. With no siblings of her own, she couldn't imagine what that would be like.

When they reached the château, they didn't get out. Anelise didn't move either because she and Nic planned to drive to the church to see the bishop. That was the whole point of her coming here. She leaned back and closed her eyes, enjoying the light breeze through her open window while she waited.

When she felt a lingering kiss on her lips that she wanted to go on and on, she thought she'd been dreaming and opened her eyes. The breathtaking man who stood there was no dream. Her heart quaked.

"Wake up, sleeping beauty. We've a call to make on the bishop."

"Nic—" The car clock revealed she'd been asleep more than an hour. She moved over to the other seat so he could get in and start the car. "Tell me everything!"

"I will after our visit. Do you need to freshen up in the château first?"

"No, thank you. I'm fine. Even if I weren't, I'm dying to know what the bishop will say."

"You and me both."

After a two-minute ride, they reached the church. Nic walked her into the bishop's office. "Come all the way in and sit down. I'm glad you're here."

"We are too, Your Reverence." He pulled the final documents out of his briefcase and laid them on the desk, then he gripped her hand. She loved it whenever he touched her. The bishop put on his glasses and looked everything over for a long time.

"You've been very thorough. These superb drawings of the new hotel and hospital preserve the majesty of the original church. I also see the area for the bovine research center. Interesting."

"We need more of them. New diseases spring up and always will."

"I'm intrigued you've given this so much thought."

Anelise sat forward. "My fiancé has always had a dream of being a research scientist."

The bishop smiled and put down the papers. "Well, my son, maybe your dream can come true indirectly." She felt Nic's tension.

"Everything looks in legal order. I've been given permission to tell you that the property is yours upon this signing."

Oh, Nic—

The bishop put his signature and seal on the paper next to Nic's.

No matter the bad news from Raoul, this was a glorious day. She knew Nic was overcome and she squeezed his hand harder.

"My father will see this and be able to die with some peace."

"Some?" the older priest inquired. "What are you saying?"

"As you know, Jean-Louis has been gone these past ten years."

"Ah, yes. I'm sorry for his suffering."

"You've relieved a lot of it with this signing. The family can't thank you enough."

"Before you leave, I'd like to give you something that belonged to your mother's brother in the seminary. After your father came to us wanting to help rebuild the church in honor of him, I sent for this little book found in his belongings.

"Inside the cover he wrote words of a quote that will be precious to your father. It says, 'If my tongue cannot say in every moment that I love You, I want my heart to repeat it to You as often as I draw breath.'"

He handed the slim book to Nic. It was another moment she'd never forget as her heart streamed into Nic's.

After they left the church and got in the car, he turned to her. "Didn't I tell you that you were my good luck charm?"

"I wish I could fix all the other worries troubling you. Please tell me."

"Where to start."

"That bad?"

"Afraid so."

"Let's get the worst over with first."

Nic cleared his throat. "Claude called Raoul yesterday afternoon. He finally heard from a man who told him Jean-Louis was discharged from the army for multiple illnesses over two weeks ago."

"Multiple? How awful."

"He left his deployment in Africa and there's been no trace of him since. The doctors didn't give him much hope for surviving. He could be anywhere, but Claude won't stop looking for him."

This was too much. "I'm so sorry."

"It's all right, Anelise. Our family has a more immediate problem."

"What else is there?" She sat back, still trying to deal with the terrible news.

"Remember when I told you this area has been plagued with what you could call vendettas?"

She feared what was coming. "Yes."

"The torching of the monastery was only the beginning. Since then there have been a number of unexplained incidents affecting our family. Last night it happened again when someone lit one of the barns on fire. Thankfully some of the workers caught it from spreading in time."

"Nic—I can't believe it. Why do you think it happened?"

"I can tell you exactly why and who did it, but I'd rather talk after we get home." He started the car again.

This man she loved was sailing into rough waters all right.

Soon they reached the château and he parked the car. "Let's go upstairs to my suite where we can be private."

He hustled her inside before anyone saw them. After they entered his bedroom, he put a hand on her arm. She wanted to be more than a comfort to him. She wanted the right to crush him in *her* arms. "If you weren't here with me right now, Anelise, I'd lose my mind."

Not you, Nic. She'd never known anyone who could handle everything the way he did.

"Do you need something to eat first, Anelise?"

She shook her head. "I'm not hungry yet, but maybe you are. That was a big meal on the plane. I just want to freshen up."

"The bathroom is right through that door."

"Thank you, Nic."

He walked over to the window and looked out on the estate while he waited for her.

"Tell me what you learned from Raoul." She'd come back in the room.

Nic turned to her. "The *grange* is the headquarters for all estate business. He has been there in meetings with the heads of the different services. Only one man didn't show up."

"You say you know the name of this arsonist?"

He nodded. "Old man Dumotte. He's the one in charge of the dairy." After a silence on her part, he said, "I can hear your mind working, Anelise."

She sat down on a nearby chair. "I have

a hunch this has everything to do with your brother taking over."

"The truth is, Dumotte never liked our *oncle* Raimond. He's too much of a reminder of Papa and I know Dumotte secretly detests him."

"Why?"

"Dumotte is a man of strong principles that don't fall in line with the way Causcelles think and run business. He barely tolerated our *oncle*, but Raoul represents our father, the man he's despised for many decades. For Raoul to show up from Paris to take over the estate has pushed him over the top. Dumotte can't handle it and had to do something destructive to let us all know how unhappy he is."

"So the barn fire is his latest declaration of war. Poor Raoul. To have to come home to a hornet's nest when there's so much sadness over your *oncle*'s illness is a nightmare."

Nic put his hands on his hips in a male stance. "Even if it's ugly, Raoul won't put up with it. This is his home where he wants to be and work, his birthright. All the estate workers love him. He'll never want to be anywhere else again."

"Yet the situation couldn't be good for

your father when he hears about the fire. What can be done about Dumotte? He's a danger to everyone with his mindset."

"For the time being my brother will put him under surveillance. He's the one with the authority and the only person capable of taking charge with Raimond so ill. If he has to, he'll relieve Dumotte of his duties at the dairy."

"Don't you think if that happens he'll come after Raoul and try to get rid of him? You know what I mean."

"Of course, and knowing that man, he'll fight to the death to keep that job. He has money to hire an attorney."

"Oh, Nic—the man sounds dangerously unstable."

"True, and anything could happen if he's thwarted, but Raoul is taking this in stages."

He felt her searching gaze. "What are you going to do?"

"I can't do anything for Raoul at the moment, so I'm working on a plan for my own life."

He saw a look of anxiety enter those fabulous sapphire eyes. "What are you saying?"

"I'd like to run the Causcelle hospital research centers that are going to be built. The first one will be here, obviously. You weren't far off when you told the bishop it was my dream. With that signed document from the bishop, I'm thinking of moving here permanently."

She seemed to be in shock. "But who will run the hotel division in Paris? There's no one like you."

"As I told you earlier, you could run everything until I have found a successor, Anelise. You're phenomenal."

She slid off the chair. "Your faith in me is astonishing, but… I have my own plans too. Your mind seems to be all over the place right now."

"It's that kind of day. If you truly aren't interested, I have lots of second and third cousins who'd give anything to live in Paris and take my job. And right now I'm getting hungry. Let's grab a bite somewhere. After that I'll show you the place on the property where I want to build my own home. Then we'll leave for the airport."

She shook her head. "What has come over you?"

"Illumination."

"Do you know what kind of house you want?"

"Yes. Something very modern with lots of windows surrounded by nature where children can play and climb trees right outside."

Her face lit up. "I can't imagine anything more wonderful."

"If I do marry, it's possible I'll be the father of triplet girls or boys. And I'll make sure they dress the way they want, figure out their own hair styles, let them explore whatever interests them, choose their own way to make a living in life. I never want them to believe I only think of them as a set."

"Is that what your father did?" She sounded hurt for Nic. He loved her so much for caring that he was in a constant state of pain.

"No, not Papa. It was other people and the media who made us feel like monkeys in a zoo."

Her eyes moistened. "I offended you when I told you how much I loved that photo of the three of you. I'm sorry."

"As I told you before, I was surprised Papa showed it to you, but I wasn't offended. My point is, if I have triplets, I'll want them to know I see each of them as an individual. But the last time I checked, the chances of my children being triplets was one in ten thousand pregnancies."

"Wouldn't it be something if you really did have triplets?"

"It might be fun to find out." He couldn't think about anything but Anelise and having a life with her. "Since we're flying back to Paris in a little while, let's get going now."

Before long he drove them to a café for cassoulet. After the delicious meal, they reached the spot he'd always envisioned for his home. He gave her his vision of everything. They walked around while he watched her expressions. Her eyes shone like stars the whole time. In his gut he knew she loved his ideas too, but it was growing late.

He glanced at his watch. "I'm afraid we've got to hurry."

"Aren't you going to tell your father what happened with the bishop before we leave?"

"Not today. Right now Papa is having to deal with Raimond's illness. They were very close."

"Of course."

"Tomorrow morning I'll fly back here. Raoul and I will spend time talking everything over with him. The news from the bishop will be first thing I'll tell him. Then we'll explain that Claude has heard Jean-Louis was deployed to a new place a few days ago. It'll be a lie because we don't want him to know he was discharged for being seriously ill. Before long Claude will know the location of our brother. We'll reach out to him and learn the truth."

"That's as good an explanation as any," she murmured. "I hope Claude has more information soon. This has to be so hard on all of you. But your good news will make him so happy."

Only one thing could make Nic happier. First, he had to tell her he wanted her for his wife, then pray for the right answer back.

CHAPTER TEN

FOUR O'CLOCK IN the morning and Anelise had never been wider awake. Nic would be leaving at five for the airport. He wouldn't be back to Paris for a few days or even longer. No doubt he and his brother would develop a strategy to deal with Dumotte and try to comfort their father.

She knew Nic depended on her to be in the office and take care of business. His idea that she could run things had to be the most preposterous assumption she'd ever heard. Her mind replayed a part of their conversation.

You take one look at a project and see the merits as well as the flaws. Ever heard of Tom Brady? He looks at the field and knows where he's going to throw the ball before anyone else has even thought about it.

Nic's over-the-top flattery had been ridiculous. But a dark chill had settled over her when he'd said he was working on a plan for his own life. Nothing could have sent her a clearer signal. She needed to make a life for herself as far away from Nic as possible.

The idea that she could go on working for the corporation would be torture beyond comprehension. He'd be living happily in La Racineuse running his research center and building a home. And she? She'd live the rest of her life in the *palais* doing what? Being the head of the hotel division? She'd known pain at Andre's death, but this would represent death on a totally deeper level.

She flung off the covers and packed up her belongings, waiting for Nic to be gone. After showering, she dressed, put her hair back with a clip and went down to the car with her bag and briefcase. The drive to the office was the shortest one in existence.

Within an hour she'd asked for her desk and equipment to be taken back to her former office. Once organized, she sat at Nic's desk and went through the four files that she'd been given to work on. By that time, Helene, Serge and George had reported for work. She phoned the three of them to come into the office for a meeting.

"Thanks for joining me. As you know, Nic

has asked me to be on top of things while he's away, which could be for a few days or even a week. But I should tell you now that I'll be leaving the corporation for good. This is my last day."

Shock broke out on their faces.

"My reasons are personal. I've lost my fiancé and can't cope." It was only the truth. "I hope that answers your questions."

They averted their eyes.

"I know how much Nic values the three of you. He's assured me you could all run this office beautifully forever without him. I believe it. I've gone through the cases assigned to me. Since today will be my last, is there one case any of you are working on that needs some legwork done? I'd appreciate being given something that will take me out of the office and keep me busy."

George leaned forward in the chair. "Louis had been looking at a school out in Fontainebleau. Because of flooding, it's up for sale in the classy part of town. He believes it could be converted into an appealing hotel. Of course, a visit to the engineers must be made before any more action is warranted."

"That's exactly what I'd love to do."

George handed her the file. "It's yours."

She looked inside. "I'll make a copy of this to take with me. I think I'll go to the Loizeau Engineering firm first. If I leave now, it will get done sooner. I'll fax you all the information I find. Thank you so much for everything."

"We'll miss you," George spoke for them before they got up. Both Helene and Serge told her they were sorry she was leaving.

She eyed each one of them. "I'll never forget my time here. You've all been wonderful to me."

As soon as they walked out, she made a copy of the file. Once she'd searched for addresses and phone numbers, she made notations and put the copy in her briefcase. After leaving the original on the desk, she picked up her briefcase and left the office through the elevator to the back entrance.

Once she'd reached her car in the parking lot, she took off for the town of Fontainebleau. No place in France was more beautiful with its forest and the exquisite château that had housed the kings of France.

At the Loizeau Engineering office, the secretary told her to wait until one of the men could talk to her and she offered her coffee. It tasted good since she hadn't eaten breakfast.

Halfway through her drink, an attractive, sandy-haired man came out to the front desk. The secretary said something and he looked over at Anelise. His blue eyes swept over her with male interest as he walked toward her.

"Mademoiselle Lavigny? You're the attorney from Causcelle Hotels—the one engaged to Nicolas Causcelle. I saw you on TV."

"Yes and yes."

"This is amazing! I'm Philippe Boiteux. I thought it was you when I first saw you, but you're wearing your hair back."

"Looks can be deceiving."

He smiled, revealing his dimples. They reminded her of Andre. She hadn't thought of him for what seemed like forever, but she felt no pain. Nic had cured her. "Follow me to my office."

She did his bidding. Once inside, she handed him the assessment done by the seller. "We want another assessment about the flooding at this school and why it happened before we move forward on anything. Does your firm have time to do this for us?"

"I'll do it now."

"That's very kind of you."

"Why don't we drive over to the school."

"Thank you. I'll meet you there."

She found the address on her car's GPS and drove there. The two-story school had a definite charm. Anelise could understand why Louis had been interested. What a shame there'd been a flood.

The engineer's van pulled up next to her and he waved. "I'll go in and investigate the problem. I estimate it will take me two hours."

"Good. I have an errand to run, but I'll be back. Thanks again."

His blue eyes smiled. Nic had constituted her world so completely, she'd forgotten that other men existed. Out of all the millions of them in the world, why had she happened to meet the one who could never be replaced?

Since she wasn't ready to tell her parents anything yet, she needed to find a place to sleep tonight. After driving around for a while, she found what she wanted at the L'Aigle Noir Hotel and registered there. Not until she drove back to the school around six did she realize the fifteenth-century mansion hotel near the Château de Fontainebleau reminded her of Nic's home at La Racineuse.

Philippe Boiteux was waiting for her outside his van when she drove up. "I'm so sorry. I hope I didn't you keep you waiting too long."

"No problem. I just came out."

"What's the verdict?"

"All the pipes need to be replaced. It's a costly job and all the landscaping will have to be redone. If your client is willing to pay for it, the work can be done." He handed her his worksheet.

"I can't thank you enough. My client will take a look at this and make a decision. If it's a go-ahead, he'll get in touch with you."

"It's been a pleasure to meet you. I'll probably see you and your fiancé again on TV."

She didn't plan on any journalist filming her with Nic again. *"Au revoir et merci."*

Right now she wanted to go to the hotel and watch something ridiculous on TV until she fell into mindless asleep. She would turn off her phone. Tomorrow would be the beginning of the rest of her life.

Nic said good-night to the family and went upstairs. He needed to hear Anelise's voice and let her know he was coming back to Paris in the morning. to hell with it being too soon to ask her to marry him. No more waiting. One day away from her was too much.

To his chagrin his call went to her voice mail. He left a message and waited for her to phone him back. Nothing. That was odd.

He tried texting her, then turned to email. No response.

It had grown late, but he called her parents. Maybe she'd gone there to sleep. Her mother answered. "Oh, Nic—"

"Forgive me for disturbing you. I'm trying to find Anelise. She isn't answering her phone or messages."

"I'm afraid she's not here. Maybe after she got back to the hotel she fell asleep."

Maybe... "Have you heard from her today?"

"No. She doesn't always call every day."

"I'm probably worried about nothing. I'll keep looking for her. Call me if you hear anything. I'll do the same."

"Of course, Nic."

He rang off and called Guy at the *palais*. He'd be back from vacation by now. "*Eh bien*, Nicolas. How can I help?"

"Have you seen Anelise?"

"*Oui*. She left at seven this morning in her car."

Nic blinked in surprise. She liked to walk to work. "Thanks for the information." He hung up and phoned George Delong.

"Nicolas?"

"I'm sorry to be calling this late, but I've got to talk to Anelise and can't reach her. When did she go home from the office today?"

"Around noon."

"Noon? I'm talking about when she left work for the day."

"That's what I'm telling you. She planned to check out an engineering firm. We need an assessment for that school out in Fontaine-bleau your father thought of purchasing. The one with the flooding problem."

He grimaced. "But I don't understand why she didn't return to work later."

"I think I do. Since today was her last, she would have no reason. She told us she would fax—"

"What do you mean *last* day?" he broke in on him in a panic.

"Anelise is a professional, Nic. She called us into a meeting and let us know straight out why. We know it's a blow. She's been a real asset, but the poor girl is suffering."

"George—what in blazes are you talking about?"

"You don't need to pretend with me. She told us she just couldn't cope since losing her fiancé. We understood."

The phone slipped from Nic's hand. He felt like a mountain had just buried him alive. "George?" he cried after grabbing it off the floor. "What engineering firm did she consult?" He had to find her!

"Loizeau Engineering, I believe."

"Thank you."

He was frantic, but it was after midnight, and he couldn't fly to Paris until early morning. *Anelise? Where are you? What's going on with you?*

His pilot flew him out the next morning, but there was a delay. Once back in Paris he went home to an empty suite. As soon as Loizeau Engineering answered their phone at one, he called them. The secretary said the man he needed to talk to was on a conference call. Nic had to wait close to an hour before he was put through to a Philippe Boiteux.

"Monsieur Causcelle? The secretary said you were on the line. I'm sorry I couldn't get back to you sooner. Have you already made a decision about the work on that school's pipe system?"

"Not yet." He broke out in a cold sweat. "I understand my fiancée worked with you yesterday. When was the last time you saw her? This is vitally important."

"She's a lovely woman." Nic's lips thinned. "I finished my investigation at six, then we both went our separate ways."

"Do you have any idea where she might have gone?"

"None. What's wrong, monsieur?"

"I'm not sure," he lied. "Thank you very much for your time."

He felt like walking death as he paced the floor of the salon. No one had phoned to tell him anything. There'd been no word from Anelise. Desperate to do something, he phoned Claude, who didn't call him back for an hour.

"Thank you for returning my call. As I told you on the phone, my fiancée is missing and I need help."

"You think this has something to do with Babette Lafrenière?"

"No. This is personal."

"If you're sure."

"Positive." This had to do with her former fiancé.

"Give me a description of her car and license plate."

"One moment. The license is in her work information on my computer." He rushed in the bedroom to get it, then got back on the phone with Claude. "I can never thank you enough."

"I'll get the police right on it."

His eyes closed tightly for a moment. "Like I said, name your price."

After hearing the click, Nic called her parents again. Her father answered immediately. "My wife's on the line with us. Any news yet, Nic?" They were worried sick too.

"Did you know that she resigned to the office staff yesterday morning without telling me?"

"What?" Her father sounded shocked. "She would never do that."

"But she did. I can't find her anywhere, and I've got the police working on it. Hugo? Does Anelise have a favorite place where she goes sometimes? You know what I mean."

"Not that I can think of."

"Nic?" his wife chimed in. "Did she tell

your staff why she was leaving the corporation?"

"Yes." He'd never been in more agony.
"She said she couldn't cope since losing her
fiancé."

"That's very interesting. Which fiancé was
she talking about, Nic?"

"Andre, of course."

"Fiddlesticks. She confided in me about
the night of your public engagement. She
said that riding up to the top of the Eiffel
Tower with you was the most transforming
moment of her life. She claimed she could
have stayed there with you forever. Later
when you showed up in Orleans at my mother's home, she had those same stars in her
eyes and darted off with you so fast we all
laughed. What's going on with you two?"

He sucked in his breath. "I'm in love with
her."

"Have you told her that?"

"I wanted to ask her to marry me from day
one, but I didn't think she would believe me."

"You're not like your father after all,"
Hugo blurted. "Don't you think it's about
time she knew the truth so we can all get
some sleep?" Hugo had hit him where it hurt,
but Anne laughed.

"You've given me an idea. Bless you. I'll get back to you."

He rang off and raced out to his car. Before long the *Tour Eiffel* came into view. Could it be true she'd been suffering all this time too? Was it possible she'd gone there today to relive the magic of the moment when they'd fallen in love?"

The crowded parking lot aggravated him. He found the first spot available and hurried into the electric elevator. Maybe she was in the restaurant looking out at the view.

Marcel saw him the second he walked in the room and ran over to him. "Ah, you must be looking for your beautiful fiancée. She came in for a while, then left to go to the observation area."

Nic hugged him, so thankful for this news he couldn't find words. In the next breath he hurried out to reach the other level. There was always a crowd of people, but Anelise stood out from everyone else. Her long hair, her bewitching profile and figure robbed him of breath. He drew closer and noticed she still wore the ring.

"Anelise?" She wheeled around and stared at him like he were an apparition. "You need to come home with me now."

"H-how did you know I was here?" she stammered.

"I'll tell you later. Right now the police are looking for your car. I need to let them and your parents know I've found you."

"But—"

"No buts, *mon amour.*"

He threw his arm around her shoulders and walked her over to the elevator that would take them below. "You've been one difficult runaway to find. Thank heaven I've come to the end of my search."

"I thought you weren't coming home for a few more days."

They reached his car and he helped her in. "My plans changed. Everything changed the moment I met you."

When he climbed behind the wheel, he messaged her parents and Claude that all was well. He also sent a message to the kitchen to prepare a lavish dinner and bring it to his suite. Finally he messaged Pierre to arrange for someone to pick up her Peugeot and return it to the *palais* parking.

Turning to her, he said, "Your car will be back shortly. All that matters now is that we're together."

"But we're not really together," she cried as Nic drove them home.

"Oh, yes we are! What I don't understand is why you didn't answer my phone calls or messages. And where did you stay last night? I want to hear your explanations once we're in our suite."

Nic's suite, not hers. Arguing with him proved to be impossible. She walked in the salon and sat down on a chair.

He followed and removed his suit jacket, tossing it on the end of the couch. "I'm waiting for answers, Anelise."

"I stayed at the L'Aigle Noir in Fontainebleau and didn't want to be disturbed."

"Not even by your boss?"

"I was too tired last night to do anything but sleep."

"What if I'd been your husband? Would you have done the same thing to me?"

"Don't be absurd. Haven't you figured it out yet? I've enjoyed being one of the attorneys, but I don't want to be the CEO of anything!"

"I don't want that for you either. I've got something else in mind for both of us."

Her head lifted. "What are you saying?"

"I want to be your husband. A few days ago, I obtained permission to marry you at church without having to wait the usual three weeks. All you have to do is say yes."

Her heart almost collapsed on itself. "Please be serious, Nic. I can't take this any longer."

"Do you think I can? I'm in love with you, Anelise. I want you for my wife." He came closer and cupped her face in his hands. "I realize you think it's too soon for me to tell you how I feel. You're about to tell me I don't know what I'm saying and that I couldn't possibly mean it. Next, you're going to say I never loved Denise, but you'd be wrong.

"I *did* love her for many reasons, but I wasn't in love with her. I didn't know if falling in love was possible for me until I met you. Now I'm aching to marry you as soon as possible. I want you in my bed day and night. I want to have children with you. I want you for my lover and soul mate. But I'm terrified that you could never love me the way you loved Andre. What if—"

Anelise pressed her mouth to his so he couldn't say another word. She stood up and threw her arms around his neck, kissing him with a passion that had been growing inside her from that first day.

Nic picked her up like a bride and lay down on the couch with her. Time lost meaning while they got to know each other in the way lovers do. She couldn't get close enough. No kiss lasted long enough.

"I want to take you to bed right now," he said against her neck. "But I want us to be married first. We might have a set of triplets and I want them to know you and I were legally wed before they came along. But I'm getting ahead of myself since you haven't told me if you'll marry me."

She pressed kisses over his handsome features before finding his mouth again. "I've been showing you how much I want to marry you ever since you asked me to go along with the fake engagement. Thank heaven for Babette, who brought us together.

"Do you honestly think I would have agreed to it if I hadn't already been smitten? The newspaper was right. I fell so hard for you, Nic Causcelle, it was scary. Yes, I'll always love the memory of Andre. He was wonderful, but that was a century ago. You and I are living in this one, and I can't wait to be your wife." More time passed as they devoured each other. Heaven on earth *did* exist.

"Cherie—" he murmured and reached for her left hand, removing the ring. "Do you remember Brigitte asking if I'd let you keep this?"

"I'll never forget that day."

"Well, she's going to find out after I ask this question. Anelise Lavigny—will you do me the honor of marrying me and making me the happiest man in existence?"

"Oh, Nic—*yes, yes!*"

He slid the ring back on and kissed her hand. "It's official now. Let's get married as soon as we can while my father is still well enough to watch the ceremony. Maybe Raimond will be able to watch too. I know your parents would rather give you away here in Paris, but—"

"Don't say another word, darling. My parents knew I was crazy about you from the beginning. I don't want to wait either."

"Your father gave me a grilling when I called them in desperation looking for you. He said I wasn't like my father after all, but he was wrong. I wanted you immediately the way my father did with my mother. But I went about it a different way by getting you to live in my suite with me first. Raoul knew what I was up to. He'd seen us together on TV and wouldn't let me forget it. As for your mother, you'll never know how grateful I am for her. She knew I was in excruciating pain and said something that helped me find you."

"What was it?"

"Apparently you confided in her about the night of our pretend engagement. Little did you know I wasn't pretending. Not any of it."

"I knew what I felt was real too, Nic. I told Maman you held me in your arms as we ascended the Tour Eiffel. You made me feel safe and cherished. With you I felt we were traveling through this glorious universe together. I admitted I'd found my heart's desire."

"Because of her, I drove there and found you!" Nic kissed her with a hunger that sent them skyrocketing.

"Darling?" she whispered when she could breathe again. "My parents will understand about the ceremony being in La Racineuse. They want to make it easy on your father."

"Why don't we call them tonight with the news and fly to La Racineuse tomorrow? We'll tell my family our plans when we get there and ask the bishop to marry us."

"Let's keep it simple and secret."

"You know my heart so well, it's a miracle."

"I can't wait to go back to La Racineuse. When we stayed in the château, I saw dozens of framed pictures on the walls on the way up to the bedrooms. The pictures of you at different ages and stages delighted me. I have a favorite."

He kept kissing her mouth. "Which one?"

"You had to be seventeen, maybe eighteen, and were driving a tractor. You wore overalls and had a smile as big as the outdoors. With longer curly hair, you were gorgeous. I fell in love with you all over again. Even if I am three years younger, if I'd met you in high school, I would have had a horrible crush on you, and you would have run from me. How many girlfriends followed you around wanting to be with you every minute? Tell me the truth."

Nic laughed, kissing every delectable feature of her face. "Dozens."

"I knew it. Anyone serious?"

"Not until business college, where I had several relationships. But none of them were strong enough to settle into anything permanent. At that time, Jean-Louis broke with father. When our schedule gave us time off from studying, Raoul usually went back to La Racineuse."

"What did *you* do?"

"I did some traveling around Europe and spent a little time in England. I discovered girls everywhere and had some good times. But I couldn't see myself being tied down to one woman. Not until I met you."

"I still can't believe you love me."

"Since the day I saw you walking toward the office, I've dreamed of holding you like this. You didn't know I was behind you."

"That explains why you opened the door to George's office so fast after I went in."

"You hooked me without even knowing it. The happy lilt in your walk, the feminine beauty of you took my breath. You had an aura different from anyone else around you. I wanted to breathe it in, if that makes sense, like I'd been put in a trance."

She kissed his neck. "I have a confession too. When I followed you down the hall to your office, I understood why the press had such a fixation on you. Talk about a presence—you had it in spades. Looking at you made me feel the way I did when I first saw Michelangelo's *David*. Your essence spoke to me the same way. I have never gotten over meeting you for the first time. To think there are three of you made like that…like gods."

"Anelise."

"So you *do* blush. That's something fun to know about you I'll treasure. I also heard your stomach grumbling. I think our dinner must be waiting."

"You know far too much about me. I love it. I love you." He crushed her to him before they got up and walked to the dining room.

The coq au vin had to be one of the best meals Anelise had eaten in years. Nic poured the wine. She'd had one glass and should have turned down a second. How foolish of her when she rarely drank at all. There was no cure for being in love with Nic, who'd made her forget about other men.

His velvety black eyes wandered over her. "Do you want more of anything?"

"Only you."

"Then let's go in the salon and dance."

Across the table, her azure eyes shimmered. "You have a romantic side to your nature."

"It's one way of making love to you. If you want to know the truth, I'm having trouble keeping my hands off you."

"You're not the only one," she murmured.

He turned on some soft rock music and pulled her into his arms. They danced for a long time, relishing the feel of each other. "Anelise," his voice throbbed. He took her back to the couch, where they got tangled together.

"Nic?" She sounded out of breath. "I keep thinking of the Seine swirling around Paris. It reminds me of the two of us with our arms wrapped around each other. I love you, Nic. So much you'll never know." She buried her face in his shoulder. "Maybe we won't be sleeping together yet, but could we stay like this until we leave for the airport in the morning?"

"You're reading my mind." His hand played with her hair. "*Mon amour?* How would you like to fly to La Racineuse tomorrow by a different mode of transportation?"

"You mean a helicopter?"

"No. I'm thinking of a certain Batmobile."

His response produced a squeal of delight he'd never heard come out of her before. "As it's the spring break, your nephews and nieces will be home. They'll die of joy and love you forever."

"I admit it'll be fun. I'll drive them around the property."

She kissed his lips. "You really do have a secret dream to be a race car driver. I have a secret too. When we whizzed to the *Tour Eiffel*, I found myself wishing we could take off for parts unknown and never come back. At least we've got tomorrow to do that."

"I'll call Raoul and bring him up to date. He'll call the bishop's secretary to make an appointment for us. Then I'll phone Pierre now so Rudi will bring the car over in the morning."

"Only one half hour with your brother tonight. I want the rest of it with me."

He laughed, then let go of her and got up from the couch. His phone rested on the coffee table. She sat up to watch him. After he hung up, she said, "We'll stop along the way for picnic food."

His eyes gleamed. "Life with you is going to be one continuous adventure."

"Especially if we have triplets. First there was that news anchor who announced the contest about our having triplets and giving the winner a Bugatti. Then you talked about triplets when you showed me the property where you wanted to build your home.

I haven't been able to think about anything else since."

"It *is* a possibility. But building our own home is a fact. I'll bring the specs I've had an architect draw up. You can look them over to your heart's content during our drive. Your input is vital. From now on everything we do will be together." He returned to the couch and pulled her on top of him. "For the rest of the night I have to hold you. Maybe by morning I'll believe this is really happening."

CHAPTER ELEVEN

A SEMI-CLOUDY DAY didn't take away from Anelise's happiness. A drive in the Bugatti gave a trip new meaning. She and Nic arrived at the family château the next day in time for lunch. With everyone assembled except Raoul, there couldn't have been a more perfect time to make their announcement. Then they'd go to the church to arrange their marriage with the bishop.

Nic stood up and reached for her hand. "Before I take all you kids for a ride, Anelise and I want you to know we're getting married as soon as possible. When our house is built out at Roselin Woods, we plan to live here in La Racineuse."

"Yay!" the children screeched in delight, then jumped to their feet to hurry outside. Anelise looked up at Nic and they both laughed. That started the adults laughing.

"Go ahead, Nic," she whispered. "Show them the time of their lives."

"I'm marrying an angel." He pressed a kiss to her lips, then hurried out of the dining room.

"I want to watch," Louis declared with a smile. "Let's all go out to the front porch."

Anelise could tell the announcement had breathed new life into Nic's father. Luca pushed him while the rest of them followed. Everyone welcomed her to the family. Their kindness thrilled her heart.

Nic took each child separately, then in groups. He zoomed around and finally let Honore drive it while Nic sat at his side. Because Anelise had never had siblings, she loved being part of this fantastic family. This would be a memorable day in Causcelle history.

"Anelise?" Louis called to her. She moved over next to him. "I've prayed for this day. My son is a different man since the moment he met you. Would that my other two boys could find the happiness that shines in my Nic's eyes. I love you for that."

"I love you too. You raised a remarkable family and saved my father from going to prison."

"So Hugo told you."

"He told me everything. If anyone is a saint, it's you. Nic is going to build that hospital with a research center out of his love for you. If we're blessed to have children and produce a son, we're naming him Louis."

He reached out and took hold of her hand. His eyes danced. "What if you have triplets?"

She chuckled. "As Nic said, it's a possibility. If they're boys, we'll name them Louis, Hugo and Raimond after your beloved brother."

His hand squeezed hers. "He's not long for this world either. His Celine is waiting for him." *Nic's mother was waiting for Louis too.*

While they both wept, the Bugatti roared into view. Honore climbed out of the driver's seat with a huge grin on his face. "He let me drive over to the *grange*. Oncle Raoul couldn't believe it!"

Nic leaned out the open window. His eyes met hers. "Now it's your turn, *mon coeur*."

"Oncle Nic said he wanted *you* to drive it."

She smiled at Honore. "I think I will."

Anelise leaned over to kiss Louis's cheek, then hurried to the car and got in behind the wheel. "I'll take us to the church now." She started the engine and they took off. "The power of this car would make anyone reckless."

"That's why we'll be returning this the second we get back to Paris. After the next turn in the road, pull over to the side."

His good mood had changed all of a sudden. She did his bidding and turned off the car. "What's wrong?"

"I went in the office to see Raoul before he came outside with me. We've hit several snags. The bishop has gone on sabbatical for six months. If we want to be married, Father Didier can do it tomorrow. Otherwise, his calendar is filled for a whole month. But here's the other problem.

"Raoul is trying to contain the tension created by Dumotte. If our marriage takes place at the church and people come, it's going to cause an uproar and Dumotte will go out of control completely."

Anelise was thinking hard. "Will the priest marry us at the château?"

"Yes."

"Tomorrow?"

"Yes. He has an opening at three in the afternoon."

"Will it be okay with Corinne?"

"She'll love it. Everyone will come together and fix food."

"Then I don't see a problem. I talked with your father while you were out joyriding. He knows the end is coming soon for him and Raimond. He's living to see you married before that happens."

Nic reached for her, pressing his forehead against hers. "There's no woman in this world like you. Do you think your parents can handle this?"

"Of course. They know I'm dying to marry you. I'll call them right now."

"Tell them I'll send a car to pick them up in the morning and drive them to the airport. When they arrive, we'll collect them in one of the cars and bring them here."

Anelise nodded and got busy. Her parents were overjoyed and would be ready first thing in the morning. She clicked off. "We need to hurry back to the château and tell Corinne and her husband what we've got planned."

"We won't be able to get away on a honeymoon for a while."

"I feel like I'm on one with you right now."

A wicked smile broke out on his unforgettable face. "That's how much you know about honeymoons. There's another part of the château that hasn't been used for a while. It's away from everyone. We'll spend our wedding night there and all the other nights when we're out here until our home is built."

"Nic—" The cry from her heart resounded in the car. She leaned across to kiss him, then she turned the key.

Three o'clock the next day couldn't come soon enough for Nic. The family had gathered in the large salon, where they were all seated. Corinne had arranged several sprays of flowers around the room. A painting of Nic's beautiful, dark-haired mother hung over the fireplace. The priest stood in front of it in his traditional wedding vestments.

That's where Nic wanted to stand with Anelise to take their vows. Neither of them had time to buy wedding clothes. He wore his dressiest business suit. She came into the salon with her father wearing an ivory *peau-de-soie* two-piece suit her mother must have brought. The pearl buttons matched the pearls she'd worn on their way to the jeweler's. He'd given her a corsage of white roses and he wore one of the roses in his lapel.

Had it only been a few weeks ago? With

the diamond on her finger, the only thing he could give her was the inscribed gold band he'd been waiting to slide on her ring finger.

Hugo walked his breathtaking daughter over to Nic before taking his place next to Anelise's attractive mother. Nic's father sat next to them in his wheelchair. Both their fathers looked smart in their best suits.

The priest cleared his throat. He looked around with a smile. "You have no idea what a lovely sight this is. To see a family like yours, young and old, all joined together to honor a favorite son and the woman he has chosen for eternity, gives me hope for this world.

"The bishop is truly sorry that he had to leave the area and couldn't marry the first Causcelle son. He sends you his blessings and his love to Louis and Raimond for all they've done for the community and France itself. We're aware of Raimond still being in the hospital and pray for him.

"Nic? Anelise? If you'll come closer holding hands, we'll get you united the way you want to be. I'll keep this short and sweet the way that I've been asked to do." He sent Nic a private message.

Father Didier was a good man. Nic grasped

her hand and they stepped closer to him. "Nicolas Ronfleur Causcelle, do you take this woman Anelise Mattice Lavigny, to be your lawfully wedded wife? Do you promise to love and cherish her forever, through good and bad, always keeping her in your heart?"

"I do."

"Anelise Mattice Lavigny, do you promise to love and cherish Nicolas Ronfleur Causcelle forever, through good and bad, always keeping him in your heart?"

"I do," she said with a tremor in her voice.

"Then by the power vested in me, I now pronounce you man and wife. You may kiss your bride once you've exchanged rings."

Nic stared into her eyes as he pulled the gold band out of his pocket and slid it on her finger next to the diamond. Her face glowed before she did something he didn't expect. She reached for his left hand and slid a gold band with a black solitaire diamond on his finger.

"Nicolas? The bride asked me to tell you that you've already lived up to the meaning of the stone that promises to be trustworthy, honest and perfect."

After hearing those words, Nic couldn't think, let alone swallow. Her beautiful face swam before his eyes. He gathered her in his arms and kissed her with his heart and soul, forgetting all else.

Maybe he'd died and gone to heaven with her. That's what it felt like. When he finally came to and lifted his head, he realized they were alone in the salon. Everyone had left quietly and gone into the dining room.

"Oh, Nic—I'm so embarrassed." She hid her face in his shoulder.

"Let's do this right and go upstairs, *mon epouse*."

"Yes, please."

In the next instant he picked up his bride and carried her through the house and up the stairs. While she kissed him, he swept them down the hall to the wing of the château prepared for them. Once inside the suite, he lowered her to the floor and closed the door, pressing her against it.

"When did you get me my ring?" he asked against her lips.

"I called Xan yesterday and told her what I wanted. I asked her to courier it to my parents. She's amazing."

"My ring is amazing. I love it."

"I love mine too."

They began removing their clothes, breathlessly kissing each other at the same time. Nic had never known desire like this. He helped remove her pearl necklace and earrings, putting them on the nearby dresser.

Like before, he picked her up and carried her to the king-size bed, where he followed her down. She kissed his jaw. "I'll love that priest forever for marrying us so fast."

"I'll love *you* forever," he half growled against her tender throat. The age-old ritual began with two people madly in love and finally able to show each other how they felt. Anelise had to be the most exquisite woman on earth inside and out. He couldn't believe he'd been able to stay away from her this long.

By some miracle she loved him and made love to him in ways he didn't know existed. She'd been gifted with an incredibly generous nature. It came out in her loving. Together they soared to impossible heights.

"I adore you," she cried over and over, enveloping him in her embrace. He felt her tears of ecstasy on his skin. They mingled with his own as he rolled on top of her, coming close to devouring her.

Darkness filled the room, but nothing mattered. They'd taken each other on a trip of such sensual pleasure, he knew he'd never be the same again. Again and again throughout the night they brought each other the joy of being man and wife in every possible way.

When the light of morning filtered in through the windows, he lay there looking at the most heavenly creation imaginable. What had he ever done in his life to deserve her? His mind contemplated the years ahead with her, the endless happiness...

"Darling?" She'd opened her eyes and she reached out to stroke his face.

"How long have you been awake?"

He leaned over to kiss her luscious mouth. "Long enough to need to relive our wedding night all over again."

She pulled him closer and wrapped her arms around him. "Not in my entire life did I know I could feel this fulfilled. It's more than happiness. It's joy beyond measure being married to you, knowing we belong to each other. Never let me go."

"Just try to get away from me, *mon tresor.*"

Their excitement knew no bounds in their need to experience the ultimate with each other. Near noon, Nic realized he was human after all and needed to eat.

This time he awakened to see Anelise

lying there studying him with a lovestruck expression in her azure eyes.

"I know you're hungry, *mon mari*. So am I. My only concern is facing everyone when we go downstairs to eat."

"We have to deal with it sometime. Let's get in the shower. I've been dreaming of taking one with you. You don't know those nights I pictured you in the shower at the *palais* after you left me desolate."

"Would it shock you if I told you I hoped you'd come into my bedroom and tell me you couldn't take the separation a moment longer?"

"Now she tells me." He kissed her again.

"I thought you were hungry. If we take a shower together, it could take a couple of hours."

"You're right. Making love hasn't damaged that razor-sharp brain of yours."

"I'll hurry. Don't look at me too hard while I escape," she teased, causing Nic to explode with laughter. Quick as a wink, she slid out of bed and hurried into the bathroom.

Ten minutes later Nic grasped her hand and they went downstairs. She looked at him. "The house seems awfully quiet."

"I noticed."

They walked in the kitchen, where they found Julie drinking juice. "Oh—I'm glad you're up, Oncle Nic."

"Where is everyone?"

"I stayed behind to tell you. The hospital called in the middle of the night. Raimond passed away."

"Oh, no." Anelise put her arm around Nic. Just yesterday Louis had talked to her about his brother's numbered days.

"They all went over this morning."

"*Papa* too?"

"Yes."

"And Anelise's parents?"

She nodded. "There's sandwiches and salad here in the fridge for you from yesterday." She pulled out two covered plates. "If you want coffee, it's ready."

"Thanks, Julie. You're a sweetheart." They both sat down to eat. "Do you want to drive over to the hospital with us in a minute?"

Her face lit up. "Can I?"

"We'll make room for you."

"I'll get my purse. I left it in the other room."

When she ran out, Nic put his arm around Anelise. "We now have a funeral to plan. I'd give anything if we could track down Jean-Louis. He loved Raimond."

"This means Raoul really is in full charge. It's a miracle that we're moving here too. He'll need your support."

"As I said the other day, the family is moving into a rough sea. I need *your* support more than ever, *mon amour*. You just don't know how much."

* * * * *

Look out for the next story in the
Sons of a Parisian Dynasty trilogy,
coming soon!

And if you enjoyed this story,
check out these other great reads from
Rebecca Winters

Second Chance with His Princess
Falling for the Baldasseri Prince
Reclaiming the Prince's Heart

Available now!